Riders Of
The Silver Rim

RIDERS OF
THE SILVER RIM

★ ★ ★

BROCK & BODIE THOENE

BETHANY HOUSE PUBLISHERS
MINNEAPOLIS, MINNESOTA 55438

Copyright © 1990
Brock and Bodie Thoene
All Rights Reserved

Published by Bethany House Publishers
A Ministry of Bethany Fellowship, Inc.
6820 Auto Club Road, Minneapolis, Minnesota 55438

Printed in the United States of America

Library of Congress Cataloging-in-Publication Data

Thoene, Brock, 1952–
    Riders of the Silver Rim / Brock and Bodie Thoene.
       p. cm. — (Saga of the Sierras)
     I. Thoene, Bodie, 1951–   . II. Title. III. Series: Thoene, Brock,
1952–   Saga of the Sierras.
PS3570.H463R54   1990
813'.54—dc20   90–1062
ISBN 1–55661–099–8   CIP

To the memory of Jesse Dodson Wattenbarger,
Potsy . . .
accomplished blacksmith,
skillful stage driver
and master storyteller . . .

Books by Brock and Bodie Thoene

The Zion Covenant

Vienna Prelude
Prague Counterpoint
Munich Signature
Jerusalem Interlude

The Zion Chronicles

The Gates of Zion
A Daughter of Zion
The Return to Zion
A Light in Zion
The Key to Zion

Saga of the Sierras

The Man From Shadow Ridge
Riders of the Silver Rim

Non-Fiction

Protecting Your Income and Your Family's Future

BROCK AND BODIE THOENE have combined their skills to become a prolific writing team. Bodie's award-winning writing of the Zion Chronicles and the Zion Covenant series is supported by Brock's careful research and development. Co-authors of Saga of the Sierras, this husband and wife team has spent years researching the history and the drama of the Old West.

Their work has been acclaimed by men such as John Wayne and Louis L'Amour. With their children, Brock and Bodie live on a ranch in the Sierras, giving first-hand authenticity to settings and descriptions in this new frontier series.

PROLOGUE

He was not sure when he abandoned the blanket roll. He probably parted company with it some time after discarding his coat and before losing the empty water bottle. He had continued to carry the bottle long after its contents were gone, hoping against hope that he would soon locate a spring. Later on the loss did not seem to matter.

Even with a derby on his head, the sunlight beating down on him seemed to be a physical weight on his neck and shoulders. His back and legs ached from supporting the burden. His head felt swollen to the point of bursting, while his body seemed shrunken, aged and frail.

The sun reflected off the sand into his face, hitting him mercilessly on both cheeks as wave on wave of heat rolled over him. It was like walking into an oven. His features were baked like overdone bread, his eyes swelled to blurred slits, his lips cracked and blackened. His enlarged tongue felt like an old, dried-up stick.

He no longer perspired. His body had no more moisture to contribute to the Mojave afternoon. What sweat had dried and darkened into salty rings on his flannel shirt now gritted and chafed against his parched skin. But he did not notice anymore.

How he continued to move forward he could not have

said. The trail stretched clearly into the heat-swirled distance, but he saw only the space of his next three steps. A nagging voice in the back of his mind told him that to stop moving was to die. For a time he argued with the voice, favoring a rest, a short break, a chance to sit down. Now the effort of disputing it seemed greater than the plodding on. He was resolved to walk until he found water—or until night fell and he could no longer keep to the path.

One step became two, then three, then another and another. There was no feeling in his tormented feet; perhaps their ache just blended with the rest of his misery. Despite his constant motion, he might as well have been simply marking time. The mountains ahead came no closer, and the hills he had descended to reach the desert plain had receded to merge with a brown horizon. The salt pan which he had been crossing for what seemed like weeks now appeared bowl-shaped, curving upward all around him.

Maybe the desert really *was* beginning to curve upward; or maybe he was just losing the strength to step over the grains of sand in his way. In either case, his constant tread became a lurching shuffle, his body bent forward from the waist. As if he were walking into a gale-force wind, the heat would not let him fall. He leaned into it, embraced it, as if to straighten up would push him over backward.

He continued staggering forward until something besides the heat worked its way into his thoughts. The sound had been there for a long while without his notice, and when he did notice it, he ignored it. Finally something demanded that he seek the source of the whispering, sighing noise. He peered about him, moving his head painfully from side to side—cautiously, as if he feared it would topple from his body. Nothing around for miles seemed to have the capacity for sound, yet the sighing had moved in closer; had become a rustling.

He blinked, then stopped stock still. The dull realization dawned that he *hadn't* blinked—a shadow had passed over his path. He forced himself to lean back, painfully straightening his neck, willing his chin from his chest, sending hammer blows of pain into his back.

His face sought the sky, and through the tiny slits of his tortured eyelids he saw it momentarily darken, then brighten again. He had the fleeting thought that he was grateful for even an instant's respite from the intense rays of the sun.

Then he saw it: a buzzard flew in lazy circles over his head. Higher still, two of its feathered companions soared, banked, and spiraled. The wings of the nearest bird made the slightest whispering sound as it passed directly overhead; otherwise the three were silent.

The man bared his teeth, even though the grimace made his lips split and crack more. He raised a clenched fist over his head. A guttural croak escaped him, more from his chest than from his burning throat.

He swayed, moving in an arc counter to the circling birds. His chin, once stuck to his chest, now seemed impossible to lower. He saw rather than felt his arm fall heavily to his side. He attempted to turn his head, surprised at the involuntary action, but his whole body twisted instead, and he fell awkwardly on his side in the sand.

———

A shadow crossed his face, then returned to hover

directly above, and something rustled close by. He struggled, attempting to flail his arms to ward off the vultures. *My eyes* he thought, *they're after my eyes!* His convulsive heave produced only a shudder of his frame. *Roll over*, he pleaded with himself.

Then the stirring came again, a soft fluttering. When it stopped, a soft voice out of the shadow spoke. "You poor man! Just lie still, here's some water."

Water! Like rain the words splashed on his soul. *Water! Saved!* A delicious coolness soothed his lips. He pursed them in a sucking motion; the moisture trickled down his throat—shocking, as if he had swallowed ice.

Tiny sip followed tiny sip. Some of the cool liquid spilled over onto his eyelids, and a hand as gentle as a feather's touch soothed his ravaged cheeks. He jerked his head, trying to shout not to waste a single drop.

The voice came again, "Don't worry, there's plenty and to spare. Your poor eyes—your poor, poor eyes."

Another splash on his lips and then another on his eyes. His body began to wake up, as if missing parts were getting reattached.

"More," he managed to groan, "more."

"Yes, of course, there is more. But slowly, slowly." The voice sounded like distant, gentle chimes.

This time he felt the touch of the bottle on his lips. A moment of panic struck him. He must have the water bottle! His arms responded to his brain, flinging awkwardly together over his chest. His clawing fingers found a sleeve, an arm, then lost it. There was a startled half-cry, and the shadow over his face retreated. The water bottle dropped onto his chest, sprinkling his face even as he grasped it eagerly and upended its contents into his mouth. His eyelids parted momentarily, and he saw the most delicate features framed in a ghostly shimmering light.

Half the contents of the bottle crashed into his stomach at once and hit his wracked and twisted insides as if he had swallowed a rock. The rock became a bomb that exploded in his brain, and consciousness fled away, leaving his punished body in peace.

CHAPTER 1

From the high vantage point of a rock-strewn bluff, the old Mojave Indian chief watched the struggle of the tall white man in the strange hat against the sun and the vultures.

The old chief could see what the white man could not: the town of Garson was only a short walk from where he had fallen. He knew the miners of the Silver Rim also could look up into the sky and see the black dots of the turkey-buzzards as they swooped and circled overhead. Perhaps they would come to the sunlight from their dark hole in the ground and think a wild horse had fallen to die in the desert. Later, they would hear that one of their own had fallen. They would wag their heads in wonder that anyone had tried to cross the desert of the Mojave without water, without a horse, in headgear that wouldn't keep the sun off a prairie dog.

For a long time the Indian watched as the body of the fool was slung across the back of the mule. Perhaps the man was dead. He would be taken to Garson and buried, then. If he was still alive, it would not be long before he died. *These white men do not belong in our land,* the chief reasoned. *The spirits take revenge beneath the sun.*

As the mule was led away, the old chief turned his

eyes back toward Garson and then to the west, where his own village nestled between the cliffs of Wild Rose Canyon.

Once, his people had been fierce and proud. They had contested dominion of the western lands with the Navajo and the Apache. The coming of the white man with their repeating rifles had broken them. Now the soldiers thought so little of them that the Indians were left to fade away in the desert.

The chief knew his white neighbors would not even consider their little camp a village. A migratory band, his tribe traveled from the Sierra peaks, where they gathered pinyons for grinding into flour, to these desert canyons where they obtained maguey for making *pulque*, a venomous, fermented brew that whites would not drink. Wild Rose Canyon was more a favorite campground than a permanent settlement.

Chief Pitahaya sighed deeply. *I am only half a ruler now*, he thought with sorrow.

They had a miserable existence, their old glory gone. The whites despised them, and they were an easy prey to white diseases and vices. Some Indians would even barter their squaws for whiskey, which they much preferred to pulque.

Chief Pitahaya argued, threatened and railed against the growing depravity of his people, but without the authority to force compliance. The white man's Indian Agents offered no assistance, and the Army said it was no business of theirs. There was no law in the desert.

The Chief watched the dust stirred by the little mule while he thought what must be done. He closed his eyes and considered the frailty of these white intruders. *What we need,* he whispered to the spirits, *is a good war. What pride we had in the days of my youth when a call to punish the Membreno horse-eaters would be answered by two hundred strong warriors! Even when the whites came to our sands, we made them go everywhere in companies of fifty for safety. And many were the fifty who never reached their stone lodges.*

Now look at us! the old chief mourned. *Faugh! We are too feeble to fight a determined gang of lizards. Nothing seems to stir us enough to shake off this sleep-with-open-eyes. Perhaps I was wrong when the white soldiers grew so powerful that I counseled Sihuarro to give up war. Perhaps I should have told him, "It is a good day to die."*

———————

Joshua Roberts sat bolt upright. His heart was pounding so hard that with each beat it threatened to burst out of his chest.

"Easy there, young fella," ordered a gruff voice. "You'd best lie still a mite longer."

"Longer? How long. . . ? Where? Who?" Joshua was trembling all over like an aspen in the breezes of the Sierra passes.

"For a fella pretty much cooked, you're plumb full of questions, ain't cha?" The voice was amused. "Lie down 'fore you shake the bed apart."

Joshua obliged. It wasn't difficult to see the wisdom of the advice, especially since he had to squeeze his eyes shut to make the room stop spinning. When he opened them again, he found himself staring at a patched canvas roof strung over a frame of mismatched wooden slats.

He was lying on a cot in someone's tent, but he could not remember how he had gotten there. He touched his face—gingerly—and noticed that the skin felt thick and leathery. The swelling around his eyes had gone down, and his tongue seemed to be in working order again.

A round, bearded face leaned into his view. Bright blue eyes peered out from lines and crevices which mirrored the desert landscape. The old man looked to Josh as if he had been carved from the desert floor and brought to life. Curly gray hair escaped from a crushed and shapeless felt hat and blended into a curly gray beard. The beard was clipped short around his jaw. He was dressed peculiarly in red flannel long-johns, stained with sweat. He was caked with a layer of dust from his hat to his toes.

Joshua was trembling with cold. How had he come to be in a place so cold, when the last thing in his memory was the searing heat?

"Who are you?" he managed to ask. "And where am I?"

The old man spread another blanket over him. "More questions, eh? Why don't cha save them questions for later and concentrate on breathin' first?" The dusty face split into an enormous grin. The leathery skin folded into a thousand fine lines, as if life here had eroded away his youth.

Again Joshua touched his own face. He wondered if he looked like the man.

"Please," he whispered with a shudder. "How long have I been here?"

"Well, for three days you been out of your skull, boy. Ravin' on 'bout this 'n that—now and then you'd haul off and yell, *My eyes! They're after my eyes!*"

Joshua nodded grimly as waves of the horrid memory flooded through him. "It was the vultures. I thought they were going to pluck my eyes out."

The old man shook his head. "It like to clabber my blood the way you was goin' on. Plumb loco."

"There *were* vultures. And then the lady. . . ." He stopped abruptly and struggled to sit up again. "Where is she?"

The old man stepped back warily. "Are you fixin' to rave some more, boy? There ain't nobody here but you 'n me."

Joshua let his head fall back. "I'm sure of it . . . there *was* a woman, a beautiful woman . . . just after I pitched over in the sand. Thought I was a goner, but she gave me a drink. I'd like to thank her."

"There ain't nobody here besides us two, unless you count Jenny out yonder." He jerked a thumb toward the open tent flap. "She's a gal all right, but she ain't no lady."

Joshua carefully propped himself up on his elbow. Through the flap he could see a little mule with her head drooping and her eyes half-closed in the early morning light.

"But I saw a lady—I even touched her arm." The vision in his mind was strong.

The old man shrugged and reached for a pair of mud-caked trousers that probably could have stood alone. "When I found you, I thought you was dead. Propped up against a rock like you couldn't go no further and had give up. Ain't no fine lady gonna be out in this outpost o' hell, boy."

Joshua lay still, struggling to reconstruct how he had gotten here . . . wherever *here* was. He hadn't the strength to ask more questions, and the old man set about his morning chores without offering further explanation.

Presently his host returned with a tin plate. "Sorry

it ain't more, boy. I ain't much a hand at cookin', and I ain't had time since comin' across you to get no Mexican strawberries on the fire." He thrust the plate into Joshua's hands. Two rock-hard, over-sized lumps of dough that Joshua recognized as yeast powder biscuits sat in a puddle of bacon grease.

Joshua dipped a biscuit in the fat and took a tentative bite. He was surprised to discover how good it tasted. Between mouthfuls and sips from a canteen, he listened as the old man launched into an account of himself and the last few days.

"My folks hung the name of John Springer on me. But where I'm known in these parts, folks call me Pickax. *Pick* for short. This is my digs, for now. Course, I might be forty mile away after breakfast, if I've a mind." Pick waved a stubby arm toward a lumpy sandstone rise visible across the dry wash. "You was just over that ridge yonder. Town of Garson is just up that way a piece. Fact is, I was comin' back from there with my grub when I seen you. You didn't weigh no more 'n a sack of potatoes, you was so dried up. I slung you over Jenny and brung you here."

Josh's eyes suddenly narrowed and his expression turned grim. "You meet anyone, coming from Garson? I mean—did you see a man dressed in dark clothes? Dark hat. Swarthy skin?"

"Is this another dream, boy? Ain't nobody crazy 'nough to be out in the heat of the day 'cept you and me. And I can't figure why you was out there without water."

"I *had* water. I may be a tenderfoot—" Joshua shrugged ruefully at the accuracy of this statement. "But even I knew not to start out without water. I met up with a man in Mojave who said he knew the way to the mines, and we traveled together. He said he knew a short-cut, so we turned off the road. Slept out that night. Next morning, he was gone—with both water bottles and every cent I had in the world."

Pick made a noise low in his throat like a dog walking stiff-legged toward a fight. "And then what happened, boy?"

"I figured I could follow his tracks. Figured he would head for more water. I finally struck the road I was following when you found me, but I never saw the man again."

Pick's face grew dark as Josh told him the story, and his outrage exploded. "He ain't nothin' but a murderer! Ought to be strung up pronto for doin' you that way. D'ya think you'd know him again?"

"Anywhere."

"Know his name?"

"Called himself Gates."

Pickax nodded solemnly, then after a few minutes' pondering the tale, he looked curiously at Josh. "Well, you know *my* name, and I know *his* name. But you ain't give me *your* name, boy!"

Joshua extended his hand with some effort. "My folks gave me the name Joshua Roberts," he said. "And that's what I go by. My friends call me Josh."

———

After two more days in the care of the old prospector, Joshua was able to move about again, but slowly.

On his walk across the desert, Joshua's feet had burned and blistered inside his boots. Pickax had cut away the leather and soaked his raw flesh in a bucket of precious water. In this way, Pick explained, Joshua absorbed two quarts of fluid while still unconscious.

As he regained his strength on biscuits, bacon and the beans which Pickax called "Mexican strawberries," Joshua had time to ponder the strange vision of the woman who had given him a drink. And, during the long, cold nights, he considered the thief named Gates who had left him to die.

Pickax said that the robber must have taken one look at Joshua's size and strength and known he couldn't take him any other way than by stealth. "You got the hands of a blacksmith, boy," the old man had commented.

When Josh confirmed that blacksmithing had indeed been his trade, Pickax grinned and shrugged as if he knew all along.

This last matter troubled Joshua. What might he have said about his past when he'd been out of his head? Did the old man know about the dead teamster back in Springfield? Had he pieced that part of the puzzle together?

"Men ain't got a past when they come out here," Pickax told Josh one night as he blew out the lantern. "Your life. My life. It ain't between nobody but you and the Almighty. There's no laws out here, boy. And nobody needs to know your business."

And so the terrible accident which had driven Joshua from his home and led him to this desolate land remained unspoken. The colors of his old life had been abandoned to bleach away in the sun of the Mojave. Yes, he was still Joshua Roberts, but when he looked into the cracked mirror in Pick's tent, he could find only hints of the man he'd been in Illinois.

Perhaps he had finally run far enough to escape his

memories. Maybe this place was close enough to hell that just *being here* was his atonement! With its freezing nights and searing days, the desert offered a man no comfort, no real peace.

There was no past here, Pick said. Only *Now* and the *Future*. Joshua Roberts had three things he wanted to do. Work again, find the woman who had given him water, and find the man named Gates who hadn't bothered to waste a bullet on him but who'd left him most certainly to die in the desert sun.

CHAPTER 2

Joshua's still-tender feet were sheathed in an old pair of the prospector's boots—mercifully, a size too large. He had not shaved in two weeks, and what precious water remained did not allow for washing his clothes. He wanted a bath more than anything, and although Pickax did not himself approve of baths, he informed Josh that such luxuries were indeed available in Garson.

On this morning, without warning, Pickax announced, "Goin' to Garson. Grub and water. Grab your hat if you're comin' along," he said, eying the derby a tad dubiously.

Joshua pulled on his hat and lent a feeble hand loading the empty water barrels onto Jenny's back. It was fourteen long miles to Garson. Fourteen miles to water. Joshua suddenly realized what a sacrifice the old man had made to share water and food with a half-dead stranger. And Joshua didn't have a penny to repay him.

"I'd like to find work, and pay back what I owe you," Josh said as they led the mule away from camp in the pre-dawn light.

Pick looked back at his ragged tent. "It don't matter none. I enjoy the company. You talk better'n ol' Jenny here. I'll put in a good word for you with Mister Morris

25

at the Silver Rim Mine. Maybe you can grub-stake me someday."

As they trudged over the desolate countryside, Joshua could not help imagining that he would find Gates in Garson and recover what had been stolen from him. Then he would be able to repay Pickax, buy himself some clothes and have a bath. Pick told him that he should buy a gun and learn to use it. He had never felt the need to carry a side-arm before.

Back in Springfield, few men had dared to challenge the strength in his six-foot-three frame. He had used his size to wrestle down horses protesting a shoeing. But out in the West, Pick insisted, it was prudent to carry a gun.

"There ain't never been a sheriff in Garson," Pick explained. "It ain't likely one would live too long, anyway."

He then proceeded to spend the hours of their journey telling Joshua the history of the little town. After all, he had been here looking for *The Lost Gunsight Mine* long before Garson was anything but a couple of tents and a well. It was hardly more than that now, according to Pick.

Still an hour's walk away, the little town became visible in the distance. It looked to be a ramshackle collection of wooden and canvas buildings shimmering in the heat, some more permanent than others but none very substantial. Pickax claimed you could throw a Chinaman through any of the walls, and the truth of this had been demonstrated more than once.

For all its flimsy construction, Garson performed the necessary functions to be called a town. About half the population consisted of hard-rock miners. The other half were there to sell their wares to the miners—or was it to prey on them? Shopkeepers, saloonkeepers, bankers and card sharps, cooks, seamstresses, and ladies of easy virtue made up the citizenry that was not mining.

Garson had a chance to become a town twenty years earlier than it did, Pick explained, owing to an unusual circumstance. A French prospector named DuBois had passed through the area hoping to locate gold. He had arrived in California too late for the rush of '49 and ended up wandering through the Panamint and Argus mountains, hoping to make his pile. When he discovered that his rifle sight was broken, an Indian guide from the local band of Mojaves offered to repair it. Reasoning that if the firearm was never returned it was useless anyway, the prospector agreed. To his surprise, it was returned in perfect working order with a new bead of pure silver!

When pressed to reveal the source of the silver, the Indian became frightened and fled. DuBois searched the canyons unsuccessfully until his water ran low and forced him to a more hospitable area. He never returned—partly because of the harsh landscape, but more probably because the lure of gold was so much stronger than silver.

Pick recalled that over the years the legend of The Lost Gunsight Mine was told, retold and embellished, or scoffed at. Occasionally it was searched for, but never successfully.

Then the gold began to play out. The placer mine's heyday was done in California, and mining began to be run by the big money moguls who could afford the equipment for underground operations. It seemed that lone prospectors had lost the chance to strike it rich— lost it, that is, until the wealth of the Comstock lode was trumpeted around the camps. Then "*Silver!*" became the cry.

The fact that fabulous wealth could be found in parched, arid lands like those of Virginia City, Nevada, miles from running water, gave the tales of The Lost Gunsight new credibility. When Pick prospected in the area, he found silver-bearing ore even if he didn't find lumps of silver sticking out of the walls of an ancient Indian tunnel.

Just as important, the returning prospectors found water! Drilling a test hole, they were startled to find a water table at only twenty feet. Without ever coming to the surface, an underground stream was gurgling its way to the salt flats of the desert floor.

Overnight a tent city sprang up, and soon after came a parade of merchants to see to the miner's needs. How the town came to be called Garson, Pick did not know for certain, but it's likely that it was an attempt to call it Garçon, in honor of the Frenchman DuBois. By 1875 it didn't matter what anyone called it; fifteen hundred souls called it *home*.

Even if their clothing was the same, the miners were distinguishable from the merchants by the speed of their activities. The miners were either in a hurry to spend their money, lose it at the card tables, or drink it up. The clerks, bartenders, and the town's undertaker were much more deliberate and methodical in their approach to life. Maybe the difference was in their knowing that wealth would come to them in someone else's pockets.

Garson's main street required no name because it was the only street in town. Josh noted that most of the buildings were grouped along either side of the wagon road that served as highway. The other structures comprising the town were set amid the creosote bushes just as their builders saw fit, without regard to straight lines or intersections. The businesses along the road had more semblance of permanence only by leaning together in what appeared to be mutual intoxication. The Red Dog Saloon leaned against the Tulare Hotel, which leaned against Jacobson's Hardware Store, which leaned against (and was leaned on by) Fancy Dan's Saloon and Faro Parlor.

Across the rocky street the scene was repeated, with the Kentucky Gentleman Saloon and the Chinaman's Chance providing rather alcoholic bookends to an office building housing a lawyer, a doctor, a dentist, and the Golden Bear Mining Company.

The livery stable and corral stood alone at the bottom of the dusty slope upon which the town was spread. At the top, dead center, was not a church or school but Freeman's Mortuary. Pickax explained that the saloons flanking the business district were the pillars of society, and that Freeman's commanding position at the head of the town showed how well the results of society's practices were provided for in Garson—or words to that effect.

Around these businesses, in random disorder, stood the tents and cabins of the population. The most elaborate of these consisted of two twelve-by-twelve rooms separated by a roofed open space or dog run. At the other extreme were canvas awnings covering cots and bearing grandiose names like *Sovereign of the Sierras* Hotel.

But Garson was definitely growing, and more importantly, families were starting to put down roots and a few children could be seen running through the streets.

———

Into this scene Pick led Jenny and Joshua. After turning Jenny into a corral, Pick and Josh unloaded the wooden water casks and filled them from the well that stood outside, then rolled them into the barn to keep them cooler. The essential job done, Pick turned and remarked, "What say we go see who all's in town t'day, boy? Maybe we can find you some work, like you been wantin'."

Joshua nodded, and the two walked up the slope through town. Pick pointed out the various establishments, passing judgment on the quality of their liquor and food and greeting several other miners pleasantly with his ready grin.

Joshua's city clothes and derby hat caused some second glances, but the costumes to be seen in Garson were so varied Josh soon gathered that his very presence with Pick caused as much curiosity as his dress. Josh returned their looks, searching each face for the man called Gates, but to no avail.

Pick guided him past all the businesses on the main road and turned aside into the mesquite just before Freeman's. The brush had been cleared off a space just big enough for a canvas tent to be erected.

"This here's the No Name Saloon, Josh. Pard o' mine by the name of Jersey Smith owns it. He came here as a miner but couldn't take the heat. So, he brung in a case of Who-Hit-John and set up this here tent. Somebody asked what the place was called, and he allowed as how it weren't fancy enough to have no name. Well sir, that hit the fella's funny bone, so it kinda stuck." He gestured broadly and waved Joshua through. "Welcome to Garson and the No Name."

Four tables, all of different ancestry, and fifteen assorted chairs completed the furnishings—except for a wooden counter along one wall. There were no windows, let alone mirrors or paintings. In fact, everything, including the patrons, seemed to be a uniform shade of dust. Everything, that is, except the proprietor.

"Great Caesar's Ghost!" erupted a voice from behind the counter. "Pickax, what's the meaning of this? Is it true you've found the old Gunsight after all? You're here to celebrate and share your wealth with your old friend and bosom companion?"

"Naw, Jersey, put a cork in it. If I tumbled onto that treasure vein, I sure wouldn't tell you—leastwise, not till it was registered proper and guarded."

At Jersey Smith's hurt expression Pick hurried to add, "Not that you'd jump it, understand. But you sure as shootin' couldn't keep a secret, and I don't want ever'body from the Trinity to Sonora knowin' my business."

"Ah, but I'd only wish to rejoice with you, my friend. To help you celebrate your good fortune."

Jersey Smith eyed Joshua for a brief moment, noting the tall, strong, and so-far quiet young man, while Joshua returned the gaze at an equally tall but thin man, a shock of white hair combed straight back and a small pointed white beard. Jersey's leaping green eyes seemed to be constantly moving; Joshua assessed him as a man of quick wit to match his glib tongue.

Smith broke the silence first. "And who might this strapping fellow be? Don't tell me, Pickax, you've finally parted with your hoarded wealth and hired an assistant to do your work while you supervise."

"Now, Jersey, this here is Joshua Roberts, late of Illinois. He and me run onto each other out by my place, and I brung him in to look for work. He ain't no actor fella like yourself, nor broken down old rock-hopper like me. He's skilled in the smithin' trade."

Joshua glanced at Pickax for the way he had glossed over the circumstances of their meeting, but did not offer to elaborate.

Instead he stuck out his hand and grasped that of the bartender. "I'm pleased to meet you," he said.

"The pleasure is mine, I assure you," responded the carefully modulated baritone. "Men as good as Pick are difficult to discover, and if he vouches for you, then your credentials are impeccable. What's your pleasure, gentlemen? The first is on the house in honor of a new acquaintance."

Before either Pick or Josh could reply, a slurred growl interrupted. From a table back in the shadows, a fleshy figure dressed in denim and flannel and packing a Colt Peacemaker stood and swayed slightly, then advanced to stand before Jersey Smith.

Of medium height, he wore his coal-black hair greased down to a bullet-shaped skull. Three days of black stubble grew on his face, and from the half-open shirt front, a tangled thicket of coarse black hair bristled.

At the sight of this intoxicated, menacing figure, Josh thought instantly how much like a bull he appeared. From his beefy arms to his thick neck and powerfully compact build, the man seemed a perfect image of an Angus in human form.

"What do you mean, on the house?" he slurred out. "What're you playin' up to this ol' dusty lump o' broken-down trash for? Las' time I asked you, you wouldn't even

allow me the price o' one stinkin' bottle. Me! Mike Drackett hisself! Now set 'em up, you pasty-faced ape. You kin
have the pleasure of buyin' a real man a drink!"

"Mister Drackett," replied Smith quietly, "I've told
you before that I don't extend credit, and that if you
don't care for my house rules, you may take your business elsewhere. As for my guests, I'll give them a drink
if I choose to, and I'll thank—"

Jersey got no further with his little speech because
Drackett shouted, "Shut your gob! I'll just help myself,"
and lunged across the countertop. Smith tried to dart
out of the way, but Drackett's powerful right hand
grasped the proprietor's shirt and dragged the thin man
back over the bar in one jerk. "Where's the key to your
good stuff, beanpole? I ain't gonna drink no more rot-
gut, neither. I just bet that key's 'round your neck.
Lemme see." Suspending Jersey on his toes with his
right, Drackett made as if to grasp Smith's neck with his
left.

But before he could get his fingers around the bartender's neck, he was astonished to find his left wrist
caught in a grip like a steel manacle and a second later
bent up behind his back.

Dropping the white-haired man to the earthen floor,
Drackett swung around but found himself confronting
no one. Joshua had danced around behind him, all the
while wrenching upward on Drackett's wrist.

"Hey, what the—? Come here, you, an' fight." Drackett attempted to reach Josh with his right, but stopped
abruptly with a howl of pain so intense that everyone in
earshot thought he'd been knifed.

"You're breakin' my fingers," he screamed, as Josh
coolly bent Drackett's fingers backward. "Stop! I didn't

mean nothin'. I was just havin' some fun."

"Your fun, as you call it, is not to my liking, nor to Mr. Smith's. Now, you apologize to him."

"Apologize? To that fancy—Stop! All right, I'm sorry! Sorry, you hear? Lemme go now!"

"Just you hold on to him another minute, Josh, whilst I relieve him o' this here piece." Pick slipped up and drew Drackett's Colt from the holster he wore tied low on the left and stepped back. "Right, now I reckon he's harmless enough. Let'm go."

Joshua released Drackett's arm, and the brawny man whirled around as if to resume the fight but stopped at the sight of Pickax casually waving the .45 back and forth. Drackett abruptly changed to rubbing his injured left hand and wrist, but it was plain he was controlling himself with difficulty.

"As I was saying, Mr. Drackett, in my establishment, I'll buy drinks for whomever I choose. And as for you, you need not bother coming in here again. Henceforth even your *cash* is no good here." Jersey regained some of his ruffled dignity.

Drackett looked angrily back and forth between his Peacemaker in the hands of Pickax and the haughty Jersey Smith. In transit his gaze stopped and moved upward to lock eyes with Joshua.

"Who're you, anyway?" he asked sullenly.

"Name's Roberts. Joshua Roberts. Now, don't you think you'd better do as Mr. Smith says and take your business somewhere else?"

Drackett spoke no further word, but turned his head slightly toward the side and gave a quick jerk of his chin. Without a sound, two men rose from the corner table where he had been sitting and followed him out through the tent flap.

Pickax moved to the entrance and watched as they made their way down the slope and back into town.

"By gum," he chortled, returning to stand by Josh, "ain't nobody *never* put a stopper to Mike Drackett afore, and without a gun or even an axe handle!"

"I'm genuinely grateful, Mr. Roberts," Jersey added. "That ruffian and his kind are all too ready to cause destruction and are not usually to be dissuaded."

"No matter," said Josh modestly. "Besides, he was all liquored up and didn't know what he was doing."

"Don't you believe it," offered Pick. "They's a rough string of hombres that's been hangin' about lately, an' Drackett's as bad as they come. You'd both best watch your backsides. Drackett'll not like bein' showed up. He's one who'd drygulch a fella. Now hold on to this Colt—after all, you won it fair and square."

"No, thanks, Pick; it wouldn't do me any good. I never learned how to use one. Why don't you keep it, or give it to Jersey here?"

"Tarnation, boy, don't they have no learnin' where you come from? Ain't you never heard of self-defense?"

"Joshua, let me offer you a gift and some advice," put in Jersey Smith.

"What's that, Mr. Smith?"

Reaching under the bar, he pulled out a sawed-off shotgun.

"Ever use one of these?" he asked in a whisper. Joshua and Pick moved in closer.

"Not on a man," Josh answered. "I've hunted pheasant and grouse some."

"Well, then, take it with my compliments. If you want to swap the Colt, that'll be all right too, but I'll make you a gift of the greener in any case." Jersey carefully removed the shells and reversed the stock to hand it to Josh.

"That's real nice of you, but I don't think I could drop the hammer on a man. Maybe you'd better just keep it and the pistol, too."

"No, my boy; when you think of this in the future, remember I offered not only a present but some advice as well. Here it is: A well-prepared man doesn't have to fight as often as one who is not prepared. Just the fact that you go about armed may convince some ruffian to avoid tangling with you. It's amazing how persuasive these two barrels can be, especially if one is looking into them. Remember, the evildoers we're speaking of have no qualms about shooting an unarmed man just to rob him, let alone one who they feel has shamed them. Please accept this weapon and practice with it. Then perhaps you'll have no need of it."

Joshua reflected an instant, then nodded his acceptance. "All right, then, what you say makes sense. I'll take it—the greener, you say—and thank you."

"Good. Now promise me you'll practice until you are proficient and—" He raised his voice so that all the customers looking on this scene could plainly hear. "No one will bother you unless they want to be chased out of town by a load of buckshot. You'll have to control that violent temper of yours, or it and these hair-triggers will get someone killed."

Dropping his voice again, he added with a conspiratorial wink, "Dramatic effect. It won't take long for word to get around. Before nightfall, you and this shotgun will be the terror of the county."

CHAPTER 3

Pick escorted Joshua over to the offices of the Golden Bear Mining Company, owners of the Silver Rim Mine. The Golden Bear was the largest mining company operating in Garson, which didn't say much for the others. Despite its proud and rich-sounding name, the Golden Bear was struggling, Pickax told Josh. The quality of silver ore recovered from the mine was tolerable, but since Garson had no stamp mill, the ore had to be shipped to Turbanville, a hundred miles away, to be processed.

Pick explained that the costs of shipping and processing and the increasingly difficult task of removing ore from deeper and deeper in the mountain kept the Silver Rim on the edge of closing. At the time of Joshua's arrival, the mine was producing $2000 per week in silver bricks. A third of its profit went to pay for the shipping and processing. Since the miners were paid $25 per week, this left very little earnings for its superintendent, Mr. Morris, to report.

Morris, Pick told Joshua, was an interesting man. In a rough country of shaggy, unkempt men, Morris was clean-shaven and kept his hair neatly trimmed—"a real gentleman," was Pick's assessment. He had experienced all the ups and downs of mining life, having struck it rich in '49 only to be swindled out of his claim by the collusion of a trusted partner and the claims recorder. Never one to give himself over to bitterness, Morris had struck out again into the canyons of the Mother Lode.

Pick said he'd heard that Morris had again located a rich gold claim, and this time he saw to it that his work was duly registered in his name. He remained partnerless. Later on he had sold out to the Golden Bear Mining Company, in exchange for cash, Golden Bear Stock, and a seat on their Board of Directors.

Morris had thought himself settled into a life of ease when the mining company dividend payments began to drop off. Upon investigating, he had discovered that none of the other Board members had any actual mining experience; assessments for mine improvements were eating up the profits.

Morris, according to Pick, demanded the chance to improve the situation and so was dispatched to oversee the Silver Rim Mine. He had succeeded in reducing expenses, and he still believed in the value of the mine, but it appeared that for once his luck had failed him. He hadn't yet made enough difference in production for the mine to turn the corner to prosperity.

Pick and Josh waited respectfully for Morris to finish giving instructions to one of his foremen.

"Now, Dub, I want you to see to it that the new face on the third gallery is cleared tonight. I want that drift to make twenty feet this week, so as to intercept the vein coming off of two."

"Yessir, Mr. Morris. Is that new shipment of timbers here yet?"

"No, blast it, but it will be by tomorrow if I have to go get it myself. Now go on with you." The foreman departed and as Morris looked up, a pleasant smile replaced his frown.

"Well, Pickax, come in, come in. What brings you to my office? Don't tell me you've finally decided to take me up on my offer of a position!"

"No, sir, Mr. Morris. I thank you right kindly for settin' such store by me, but the truth is, I got this here young man to see you about it."

Morris rose to his feet and stuck out his hand. "Pleased to meet you, young man. What did you say your name was?"

"My name's Joshua Roberts, Mr. Morris. I'm a smith by trade. I just came here from Illinois, and I'm anxious for work."

"Smithing, eh?" Morris stopped and appeared to be sizing up Josh much as one would choose a draft animal. "Are you a drinking man, son?"

"No, sir, I'm not—" began Josh.

Pick interrupted by snorting, "I'll say he ain't! Why, he even turned down a drink after the offer of it 'most got him killed. He disarmed Mike Drackett slick as you please and still didn't take no drink to celebrate!"

"What's this? Are you a brawler then, young man?"

Josh opened his mouth to reply, but Pick again saved him the trouble of answering. "A brawler? Shoot, he ain't no brawler, he's a genuine iron-corded set o' human manacles!" Pick proceeded to recount the events in the No Name Saloon with great gusto, while Morris nodded, raised his eyebrows and smiled occasionally.

When Pick finally subsided, Morris turned to Joshua and said, "If you are half as good as Pickax here claims, you can have an immediate position with me as a security guard. I'll pay you twenty-five dollars a week."

"No, thank you, Mr. Morris. I'll tell you what I tried to tell Pick and Mr. Smith. I'm no hand with a gun, and fighting's not my line. They seem to think I should practice up with this old scattergun, but I wouldn't care to be a guard. Don't you need a smith, sir?"

Morris shook his head as if disappointed but replied, "As it turns out, we do. Even though I've known him a long time, I've had to discharge our blacksmith just yesterday for being drunk at work. He has ruined four-hundred-dollars-worth of drills by his inattention. You can have the job, but I'm afraid the pay is only twenty dollars a week. Are you certain you wouldn't consider the guard's position?"

"No, thank you anyway, Mr. Morris. That blacksmith spot suits me right down to the ground. What time do I start?"

"Come tomorrow at seven. I'll have Dub Taylor, the general foreman who just left here, line you out."

———————

Josh found lodgings in the modest but clean Tulare Hotel. Its proprietor, Mrs. Flynn, as Irish as her name, took an immediate liking to the young man and saw to it that his cot in the dormitory-like room he shared with seven other men had a clean Navajo blanket rather than the old army-issue wool blankets which served the others. "Ten dollars a week, and two square meals a day goes with it. Leavin's can be taken for your work meal. No drinkin' nor fancy gals in my place, an' I'll have no smokin' or chew in the sleepin' room, if you please. Smokin' and chewin' is permitted in the parlor, except on Sundays."

Josh replied to each of these pronouncements with a

respectful "Yes'm" and "No'm."

"Breakfast is at six and supper is at four. Look sharp, or you'll get naught. Unless," she said, softening a little, "you come to be workin' graveyard, then I'll be savin' you some biscuits for when you come off shift—but no," she remembered, "the smith works morning tower except at need. If I want some repairs done, likely you can work out some costs, if you've a mind."

"Yes, ma'am."

"An' one mare thing," she said, her flattened "o" betraying her County Cork origins, "I run a quiet house, so's men can get their sleep. My dear departed Clancy, God rest his soul, was a miner, and he swore by good food and good rest."

———

Joshua lay awake in the dark room of the Tulare Hotel and listened to the night sounds of Garson as a cool breeze passed through the open window.

He hoped that the good food promised by Mrs. Flynn was better than the good rest she held in such high esteem! The hoots and whistles of Josh's seven snoring roommates kept sleep far from him.

The sound of a dance-hall melody emanated from Fancy Dan's Saloon. Then the sounds of hymn-singing, of all things, began to rise and fall in a strange counterpoint to the honky-tonk music.

Shall we gath'er at the Riv-er. . . .

Thar's a yel-low rose of Tex-as! I'm go-in' there to seeeeee. . . .

Among all the saloons and gambling houses there was not one church to be seen in all Garson. Yet Joshua was certain he heard church music—women's voices!

Yes! We'll gather at the Riv-er. . . .

No-body else could love her, not half as much as meeeeee. . . ."

Joshua sat up, careful not to bump the little miner from Cornwall who slept beside him. The man stirred.

"Seems the Crusaders are at it again," muttered the little man.

Josh was glad someone else was awake. "The music—" he began.

"Aye, they'll stop soon enough. There's a group of 'em. They've taken the pledge."

"The *pledge*? You mean there's a Women's Christian Temperance Union in Garson?"

"Aye," replied the weary voice. "They'd close down every saloon and bawdy house in town if they had their way. Every night a different shift of 'em sings until Fancy Dan's closes down. His place is the only saloon with a piano." He yawned. "You'll get used to it."

Joshua was smiling at the image: members of the Temperance Union singing hymns in the dark outside the town's biggest saloon. He was, himself, a man of temperance where whiskey was concerned, although he was not religious and made no attempt to awaken the conscience of a drinking man.

"Are there miners singing with them?" he asked, hearing a male voice in harmony.

"Some. And she's *even* managed to save the souls of a few of the Calico Queens!"

"*She*? She who?"

Now the Cornishman chuckled. "You haven't met her, I see. Do your utmost *not* to meet her, Mister Roberts." He rolled over. "Aye. She's tough as iron! Spotted me for the sinner I am, right away." The voice became sleepy and faded into a soft snore.

Now the music shifted to *The Battle Hymn of the Republic* as Joshua envisioned the town battle-axe leading the chorus. He would do his utmost to avoid her—*whoever* she was! Like Pick commented, his past was his business. Between him and God, he'd said.

But Pickax had not warned him about *the battle-axe*. No doubt such goings-on was one reason the old prospector chose to live fourteen miles out of town!

Joshua finally fell asleep, an amused smile on his lips, as the members of the Garson Women's Christian Temperance Union continued their musical showdown late into the night.

———

Fancy Dan's Saloon and Faro Parlor were operated by Fancy Dan McGinty. So called because of his flashy manner of dress, it was an image he not only enjoyed but fostered.

McGinty was a little over middle height and stockily built. Despite his last name, his olive skin and wavy black hair owed more to his mother's Mediterranean forebears than to his Irish father.

Early in his life, McGinty had discovered that living by his wits was preferable to using his muscles, and that it was easier to part others from their hard-earned money than to earn his own.

He lived by two mottos: *You can never have too much of wealth or power*, and *No one should be allowed to stand in your way of increasing either*.

McGinty had amassed a significant amount of capital by fleecing the miners of Virginia City, Nevada, with a crooked faro game. When he heard of the silver strike in Garson, he decided the time was ripe to invest on the

ground floor of a new opportunity. This decision to re-
locate was motivated in part by a disgruntled group of
miners who had threatened to stretch McGinty's neck.
He concluded that a change of method as well as venue
was required.

Since arriving in Garson, McGinty had risen in both
wealth and popular opinion. His saloon, if modest by the
standards of a more civilized part of the world, was op-
ulent for Garson. A real wooden building, its plank floors
were kept swept, and the genuine mahogany bar was
polished to a dull sheen. Behind the bar were signs ad-
vising miners to enjoy the free lunch and admonishing
them to write home; paper and ink supplied, gratis.

McGinty's employees were the best. He tolerated no
obvious cheating, relying instead on paid schills who
encouraged both immoderate drinking and excessive
betting. He also maintained a group of strong-arm types
who not only maintained order but saw to it that the
house got its proper share of the profits. No one working
for Dan McGinty went independent and stayed healthy
in Garson.

But for all his success, McGinty was not content. He
was steadily increasing his fortune, but what was there
to spend it on five hundred miles from nowhere? He
dreamed of returning to his hometown of San Francisco
in regal style—building a mansion on fashionable Rus-
sian Hill and mingling with the Hopkins and the Crock-
ers. This dream could not be realized, however, without
his becoming *really* rich, even fabulously wealthy. He cal-
culated that owning a top-producing silver mine would
do it.

Fate certainly seemed to be smiling on Dan McGinty.
In his clandestine recruiting efforts among the miners,

he had not hired all of them away to become schills, card sharps and bouncers. Some he conveniently left in place as informants and for other purposes as the need arose.

None of these confederates was more valuable to him than Beldad, the graveyard-shift foreman at the Silver Rim. A small, bitter man with a much-inflated opinion of himself, Beldad believed that he should have been made the general foreman of the Rim, and when he was passed over for this position he made his displeasure known around Garson.

A few dollars and the promise of elevation to his rightful place had more than won Beldad to McGinty's side. He was angry at the whole world; Mine Superintendent Morris became his convenient target, and he eagerly encouraged griping among the miners. McGinty's grand strategy called for the work in the Silver Rim to be slowed to a virtual standstill in every way possible. Fancy Dan reasoned that when Morris was shown to be a failure and the Rim near insolvency, the rest of the Board of Directors of the Golden Bear Mining Company would be pleased to unload the whole boondoggle for a very modest price.

All had been going according to plan until Beldad had brought some unexpected news to Fancy Dan. Beldad came to the back stairs leading to the second floor of Fancy Dan's Saloon. There was no reason why he could not enter the front to drink and gamble with the rest. No reason except that tonight two dozen Temperance members were singing on the sidewalk outside the saloon.

Two raps in quick succession, followed by two more, and the door was opened by McGinty himself.

"What is it, Beldad? I've got Dr. Racine, Freeman,

and the new Wells Fargo agent coming over in about twenty minutes for a little card party. Make it quick."

"Boss, you won't be thinking about cards when you hear what I've got to tell. It's bigger 'n anything."

"All right, spill it. What's this great news that can't keep?"

"You know that new gallery we're opening in the mine on level five?"

"Yes, what of it?"

"After we shot the south face last night, I was the first one back in there. Boss, we've hit it—I mean, really hit it! There's a silver vein there as wide as this room and so rich it almost glows!"

"Are you certain? Morris was positive the best chance was on three—you told me so yourself."

"I know, I know, but Morris is wrong. Five is smack spraddle of the sweetest ledge you ever saw, perfectly cased in clay and running down into the mountain. Morris could stay on three the rest of his life and never lay eyes on this."

"Have you tested a sample yet? I mean, you're not getting the 'fever,' are you?"

"Boss, listen. This ledge is shot through with blue threads—blue cables, more like! I chipped out a piece for the fire assay—and mind you, I was in a panic to get out before the men came in to see what was keeping me, so I didn't pick and choose. Boss, that bit assayed out at two thousand dollars per ton!"

"Two thousand the ton! Are you positive?"

"Absolutely certain."

McGinty grabbed the smaller man's shoulders and held him, frowning in deep thought. When at last he spoke he looked squarely into Beldad's eyes. "Not a word of this to anybody, or I swear I'll give you to the vultures piece by piece myself."

"No, no. Not a word."

"Also, this changes things. We've got to work faster. We can't take a chance on Morris discovering the ledge. If he did, Golden Bear'll never sell out and he'd have all the financing to develop a mill right here.

"We've got to speed our plans up. Do what you can to delay any further work on five while I figure out what's to be done. We've got to keep Morris so busy with everything else that he won't even have time to think about mining. Nothing must interfere now. Nothing!"

———————

Beldad exited McGinty's office by way of the back stair. He could still hear the strains of "In the Cross of Christ I Glory" competing with a raucous version of "Sweet Betsy From Pike."

A short looping walk in the darkness brought him back onto the road at an angle that suggested he was coming directly from his cabin. He was still early for the change of shift, and he saw no one on the way to the Silver Rim.

Beldad acknowledged the hoist operator with a curt, "Goin' down to three." As the wooden floor of the lift began to drop down into the blackness of the shaft, he flicked the butt of a cigarette into a mound of sand. He watched overhead as the gallows-frame, which supported the great block through which the cables ran, was briefly silhouetted against the stars. As the lift dropped further, it disappeared from his view.

Stepping off when the platform halted on the third level of the mine, Beldad glanced around. As he expected, no one was yet approaching the lift to return to the surface. He had arrived unseen.

He could hear the clang of the double-jack and drill and the sing-song cadence of the miner's picks working the face of the ore on level three.

The rumble of an approaching ore car was just becoming audible as Beldad turned sharply to his right. Near the lift was an unused *winze*—a vertical shaft that connected different levels of the mine by ladder.

Elsewhere, the winzes were in use, but this one was so near the hoist that it seldom had traffic. Beldad was able to descend by its wooden rungs all the way down to the deepest part of the Silver Rim.

Pausing at the opening of a connecting passage, Beldad listened for any human noise to accompany the clanking sound of the pump. When he judged the way to be clear, he stepped out into a chamber where a fitfully flickering lantern marked the location of the pump laboring to remove water from level five.

Nearby, on wooden skids, sat a replacement pump ready in the event that the first failed in some way.

Glancing around once more, Beldad took a wrench from one pocket of his long coat. He quickly removed the cover from the pump; then, from another pocket, he retrieved a sack of iron filings. He poured these into the mechanism and replaced the cover.

By the time Beldad repeated this process on the spare pump, the first was already making strained, complaining noises.

CHAPTER 4

At 6:30 the next morning, Josh was waiting outside the foreman's shack near the entrance to shaft number one of the Silver Rim Mine. The foreman, Dub Taylor, was just exiting from an ore car which he had ridden to the top of the shaft. He was addressing a short, stocky, bald-headed man who had come up with him.

"How do you explain that pump breaking down so fast, Win?"

"It was no breakdown, sir; it was wrongly installed, I'm thinkin'."

"Wrongly installed? But how can that be?"

"Well, sir, I canna rightly say."

"All right, then, I'll have a word with Beldad, and I'll see that Parker hears about it. He'll have to stop the work on three until we get gallery five cleared, otherwise we'll lose it."

He turned to see Joshua waiting, then pulled a Rockford dollar watch from his pocket and examined the time. "Come early your first day, eh? I like that. Mr. Morris sent word to expect you, Roberts. I'm Dub Taylor."

"Pleased to meet you, Mr. Taylor. It sounds like you're having some trouble?"

"That we are, indeed. What do you know about mining, son?" At Josh's shrug he continued, "Well, no reason why you should, blacksmithing being a lot the same for farming or mining, I guess. Anyway, these mines are deep—" He waved his hand toward shaft number one. "And the deeper we go, the more we have to fight to stay ahead of the water.

"Mr. Morris thinks the vein we're following on three is fixing to widen out into something worthwhile," he continued, "but now I've got to jerk my crews off of three till we get five pumped dry and the damage repaired." He shook his head, then smiled briefly at Joshua.

"Anyway, it's no concern of yours. Come on with me to the smithy."

Taylor led Josh up the hill a short distance behind the foreman's shack; Josh identified the smithy by the heaps of iron lying around and the glimpse of a forge through the half-open door.

Dub nudged a pile of drill bits with his foot, then said in a disgusted tone, "I don't know how much Mr. Morris may have told you about the man you're replacing."

"Well, he said he was drunk at work," Josh replied quietly.

"Drunk at work is right! And not the first time, either. But this time it wasn't a bolt cut too short or a shoe not fit properly, it was hundreds of dollars of drill bits just brought in to have the edges put back on them. Now look at them: Every one bent out of true and absolutely useless!"

Josh nodded and leaned over to look at the obviously curved metal spikes. "I can fix these," he said.

"If you can, it'll be a miracle. We need those bits sharpened to replace the ones we're using now, otherwise it brings everything to a stop to re-edge the one set. If we sent for more, it'd take two weeks for them to get here, and it's an expense we can't afford right now."

"Just let me get to it," Josh said.

Dub shrugged doubtfully but shook his hand and turned to go. "No harm in trying," he said.

"If you need anything, see Parker," Dub called over his shoulder. "He's the day shift foreman. I'll send him over to meet you."

Josh inspected the smithy with a critical eye. The slag had not been cleaned from the forge any time recently, and the floor appeared never to have been swept. Since straightening the drill bits would require a precisely-controlled fire, Josh decided to attend to the forge first. He cleared it out completely, then restacked it in a careful pyramid shape of coke built over charcoal and kindling.

A shot of coal oil, and the forge was blazing cheerfully. While Josh waited for the blaze to subside before working the bellows, he located a broom and swept out the place. Next he rounded up a variety of hammers and tongs and cleared a work bench of debris. As he was filling the tempering keg, a tall red-haired man walked up.

"I'm Parker," he announced. "Best luck with those bits, Roberts. I hear there's a peck of trouble on five, so I've got to go. I'll see you at the end of the shift." With no more conversation than that, he was gone.

Joshua worked steadily all morning. His pace was unhurried as he gave attention to each bit in turn, judging with his practiced eye when each was the exact shade of cherry-red to be reformed. His hammer made a rhythmic sound as it bounced from steel rod to anvil in a precise cadence.

As he completed the straightening of each bit, he returned it to the forge and heated the cutting tip to the white heat required to form the edge for splitting the silver ledge a hundred feet below where he stood.

The morning was heating up after the cool of the desert night. As each rod was finished, Joshua allowed himself a moment to stand in the shade of the doorway and catch a moment of breeze. From where he stood he could gaze across the valley floor west of the mining camp. Sometimes it would be obscured by dust-devils and made hazy by waves of heat. At other times it cleared for a moment—long enough for him to see the bright white reflection of an ancient, dry lake bed.

Most often his eye did not linger on the desert floor but would be drawn upward to the gray mass of the Sierras beyond. Though they were far enough away to be indistinct, an occasional peak thrust up into the morning light radiated a glistening shine off its snow-covered summit. In his mind's eye, Joshua could see an eagle turning lazy circles over those peaks, gazing down at majestic pines and redwoods reaching heavenward from rocky slopes.

Josh shook his head and sighed, then returned to his forge. By noon he had completely reshaped and sharpened all the drill bits and turned his attention to other projects he found lying about in obvious neglect. He repaired several buckets and welded the broken stem of a windlass handle. He was just debating whether to repair a broken wagon spring or straighten a pick head when a shadow fell across the work bench. Someone was standing in the doorway behind him.

Shading his eyes against the gleam of the westering sun, Josh walked toward the door to see what was wanted. A blast of whisky-laden breath almost knocked him back a pace.

"What you doin' theah?" demanded a slurred and angry voice.

"I'm the blacksmith," replied Joshua. "What can I do for you?"

"The devil you say! I'm the blacksmith heah—Big John Daniels. Now get outta my way," the man demanded, roughly shouldering his way in.

Josh had moved to the side as Daniels entered. Now that he could see better, he could tell what an enormous man Daniels was: six-foot-six, three hundred pounds, and black as night. Daniels' shiny, bald head seemed his only part not able to grow with complete success.

"Daniels, Mr. Morris told me you were let go. I'm the new smith here," said Josh simply.

"Says who?" sneered Daniels. "You gonna put me out, you little pipsqueak? Ain't nobody fires Big John. I'll go when I've a mind to, an' not sooner. Now you better skedaddle, or I'll crack yo head like an egg!"

"Listen here, Daniels, you've not been doing your job around here, and being drunk like you are now almost cost this—"

Joshua never finished the sentence, for with a roar that was probably heard in Mojave, Daniels grabbed a hammer from the work bench and charged at Josh.

Josh ducked under the blow, and a good thing too, because the descending hammer and the force behind it knocked a hole completely through the west wall of the smithy.

Josh put the forge between himself and Big John as the giant lumbered around in a clumsy circle. "Stand still an' fight, you little rat," Daniels bellowed, "or I might jes' wreck this place so's *nobody* works here." At this he seized an iron bar and, with a round-house sweep, he took out the bellows chain, dropping it crashing to the floor.

"That's enough!" shouted Joshua, and he leaped to catch the bar at the end of its swing, pinning it against the ground.

Big John struggled for a moment, attempting to free the bar from Josh's grasp. He was startled at Josh's strength and even more surprised that Josh stood up to him.

When his fuddled brain finally understood that he could not wrestle the bar away from Josh, he dropped the hold he had on it with his right hand and drew his fist back for a swing aimed at the back of Josh's head.

This was exactly what Josh had expected, and he was ready for it. Even before the blow began, Josh gave a sudden shove on the bar directly toward Daniels.

The move caught Daniels off guard; pulling on the bar with his left hand, he was not prepared to stop its sudden plunge into his mid-section.

His breath exploded with a convulsive burst, and he began panting in short gasps.

Despite his heaving, he put his head down and charged Josh. The reach of his arms and the force of his rush propelled Joshua back into the opposite wall. With a crash and a clatter that sounded as if the mountains were falling, tongs and hammers and blanks of iron for horseshoes flew from their shelves.

Big John's eyes lit up with unholy glee, and he raised both fists over his head, ready to smash them down on Joshua.

Josh threw a hard right that caught Daniels on the

jaw and rocked his head back. A left drove into the big man's rib cage just above his massive stomach, and Daniels staggered.

He lunged forward again, intending to catch Josh's neck in the crook of his arm. He knew he could squeeze until Josh's neck broke. But Josh flung both arms up quickly, threw off Big John's grasp with an upward motion, and in the same move grabbed the giant's head behind both ears.

Josh threw himself back violently, at the same time yanking Daniels' head downward with all his might and raising his right knee to meet it.

A sickening, crunching sound resulted, like the noise of a rotten tree when it falls. Daniels' nose and mouth burst like a watermelon dropped from a wagon bed, and he slumped heavily to the floor.

Josh backed up, breathing heavily, and took stock of his injuries. His shoulders and the back of his head felt like they were on fire from being jammed against the wall, but otherwise he was unhurt.

He picked up a ballpeen hammer and moved cautiously over toward Daniels. As he approached, Daniels moaned and stirred slightly, and Josh raised the hammer. Then a hissing, bubbling sound escaped the fallen giant as he exhaled a lengthy sigh from his ruined mouth and nose. Josh shuddered at the thought of further violence, and threw the hammer to the floor.

A noise at the doorway made him glance in that direction. There stood not only Parker, the day foreman, but Mr. Morris and a crowd of miners.

"Are you all right, Roberts?" asked Morris.

"Man, it looks like an earthquake hit here," commented Parker. "How did you keep from being slaughtered?"

"I just got lucky, I guess."

"Lucky, nothing!" said Parker. "Nobody has ever bested Big John in a fight, drunk or sober. Half the miners off shift came running to tell me Big John was coming with blood in his eye to wreck the place. The other half are laying odds on how many pieces you'd be found in!"

"Not *all* the others; several came to warn *me* that Daniels was on his way up here," commented Morris. "I came as fast as I could to see if we could subdue him, but here you've done it all by yourself!"

"Mr. Morris, maybe God is just looking out for me." Josh was uncomfortable with the obvious respect on the faces peering at him.

"That may be, my boy, that may be; but you were brave enough to stay and look out for mining company property when a lesser—and more sensible man, perhaps—would have run away. I want you to reconsider working as a guard for me. I'll make it thirty dollars a week."

"No thank you, Mr. Morris. I said before, I'm a smith, not a guard or a lawman."

"Well now, say, Mr. Morris," began Parker, "what are we to do with Daniels there? I mean, we don't want him to be loose when he wakes up."

Morris reflected a moment, staring at the hulk on the floor. "Say, that's right. We could . . . maybe in the . . . perhaps the basement of. . ." He stopped in consternation. "Where is there a place strong enough to hold him? We don't have a jail in this town, and if we weighted him down with enough iron to hold him, we couldn't move him ourselves. Besides, he'd tear down any place we confined him, weighted down or not."

"All right, Parker," he continued, "detail off some men to guard him." He stopped as Parker and the others who were crowded into the doorway began backing up. "Well, what is it? Are you all afraid of him? Come, come, where's your courage? Can't you put some guns on him? He wouldn't charge a hail of bullets, surely."

"It ain't just that, Mr. Morris. Sooner or later he'll have to be let go, an' he'll remember every mother's son who guarded him. Big John ain't much on thinkin', but ain't nobody can hold a candle to him for gettin' some of his own back!"

Morris paused a moment to look around the circle. "Do all of you feel that way?" he questioned. A vigorous nodding of heads was his reply.

Morris turned to Josh and found him gazing speculatively around the smithy. "And what about you, Roberts? Do you have any ideas?"

Everybody expected Josh to reply that he'd done his part already.

"Have you got a length of ore car track to spare?" he asked.

Morris glanced at Parker, who replied, "Sure, we've got a whole stack the other side of shaft number three. So what?"

Josh addressed Morris again. "And that level space that's cleared down there—" He motioned toward a vacant patch of ground behind the foreman's shack, out of sight of the road from mine to town. "The one with the pit in the middle—is that to be used for anything?"

"No," Morris answered. "It was an exploration shaft, only five or six feet deep; the clearing is to be the site of a new mine office, just as soon as we bring in the big vein, right men?"

A chorus of half-hearted affirmatives responded, but Morris ignored the lack of enthusiasm. "What have you got in mind, son?"

"I think I'd better show you. Mr. Parker, how long is one of those rails?"

"Twenty feet."

"That will work just fine. Could you get some men to bring a rail to that cleared space?"

Parker looked puzzled and glanced at Morris for approval, who nodded. Then he addressed the group of miners. "Jones, take nine men with you and bring back that rail, double quick now. All right Roberts, what next?"

Josh selected a piece of metal rod about four feet in length and handed it to Parker. "Have someone bolt this through the tie-flange of that T-rail." The men glanced at each other dubiously.

"All right," he went on, "help me drag him down to the clearing." There was a general movement backwards, which Morris attempted to stop with threats of firing. But Josh was even more convincing: "You don't want him to be loose when he comes to, do you?" There was a rush forward, and soon ten men were dragging Daniels down the short slope to where the rail rested with the cross-bar already bolted in place.

When the pit had been filled in with rocks and leveled under Josh's direction, the rail was standing upright in the center. Josh was about to ask the men to drag Daniels' still-unconscious bulk to the rail. But the miners had already guessed his intent, and in a flash Big John was seated on the ground with his legs straddling the rail and his battered face leaning up against it.

It took no time to fashion manacles and leg irons

from chains, hammering the bolts so that the chains could not be released without being cut free.

When the last stroke was completed, Josh stood and addressed Morris. "There's your jail, Mr. Morris. Even Daniels can't pull that rail free of two tons of rock, and he can't climb fourteen feet of rail trailing those chains, either."

"Brilliant, my boy, brilliant!" Morris spouted jubilantly.

Parker spoke up, "There's just one thing, Mr. Morris."

"What's that?" said Morris, who was beaming in satisfaction.

"Well, sir, I expect you'll be sending for the deputy sheriff to take charge of Big John and, well, sir, seeing as how it'll take three or four days to get him here, who's to care for Daniels meantime?"

"I thought you, or your—"

"No, sir, I don't think so. I mean, we didn't sign on as no guards, and anyway, we got some mining to do. Ain't that right, men?" This time the chorus of assent was loud and enthusiastic. No one wanted to be remembered by Big John as having been the cause of his confinement.

Joshua sighed and shook his head ruefully. "I guess it's up to me, Mr. Morris. After all, it was my idea, and here he is right in my front yard, so to speak. I'll see to him."

A relieved murmur went through the crowd, and Morris grasped Josh's hand eagerly. "Well done, my boy, well done! Now listen you men, this is the kind of spirit that will make this mine prosper and all our livelihoods will be secure. Roberts, I'm upping your pay as blacksmith to the thirty-dollar-a-week figure anyway.

"And—" He groped in his pocket and displayed a gold double-eagle. "Here's a twenty-dollar bonus!"

———

Later that evening, Josh went back to the mine property with a jug of water and a plate of beans. He told no one what his plans were and spoke to no one as he went.

Over his shoulder he carried a Navajo blanket. The sun was setting as he stopped by the foreman's shack. No one was inside, but he borrowed a lantern anyway, and when he had it burning cheerfully he stepped outside and went around the back.

Big John was still leaning against the T-rail, but a stirring let Josh know he was awake.

Josh stepped up to the edge of the filled-in pit and said, "I've brought you some supper and a blanket."

Through bruised and swollen lips, a garbled voice replied, "What makes ya think I wan' anythin' from you? All I wan' ri' now is ta git my hands 'roun yo neck and pop yo head off yo body like a cork outta a bottle."

"I figured you'd be feeling that way about now," Joshua replied evenly. "But even so, I said I'd be responsible for seeing to you, so here's food and bedding. What you do with them is up to you."

He set the plate, bottle and blanket down within reach of Daniels, but on the opposite side of the rail. Joshua then backed up slowly, taking the lantern with him. Once out of the small circle that made up Big John's cell, he turned to go.

"Hey!" shouted Daniels after him. "Ain't cha gonna leave that lantern here?"

"What for?" asked Josh. "You aren't going to be walking anywhere, and you said you didn't want anything from me, remember? Anyhow, it's company property, and I've got to return it."

"How long you gonna leave me like this? I mean, how about turnin' me loose?" he whined.

"No, I can't do that. You put yourself in this fix, and I can't get you out of it. As to how long—well, I think they've sent for some judge or other."

"A judge? That could take mos' a week! Say, don't cha know they's rattlesnakes and scorpions out here at night? What'm I s'posed to do about those?"

"Well, now, I'll tell you. If it was me, I'd wrap up good and tight in that blanket, and I'd lay real still all night and roll over real carefully come morning."

"What?! Why, you—I'll break ever bone in yo sorry carcass. I'll string yo intestines up like sausages and use yo guts for garters. I'll—"

But Big John was shouting imprecations at empty space. Josh had taken the lantern and departed.

CHAPTER 5

The next morning Josh carried a plate full of biscuits and sorghum and a jug of buttermilk with him to work.

He found Dub in the foreman's shack. Dub eyed the food and shook his head with a wry smile. "I don't envy you, even if I am sorry I missed seeing what happened yesterday. How'd you get stuck feeding that wild bull? Didn't anybody tell you he never forgets and never forgives?"

Josh grinned. "Back home my daddy taught me to break horses by keeping them tied short, and giving them fodder and drink by my own hand. That method never failed to bring around the most cantankerous, rough stock you ever saw, so I thought maybe it'd work on the same kind of human stock."

"You'll pardon me if I don't go with you to watch," said Dub. "I don't even want to be associated with you in Big John's mind. Just leave me an address of your next-of-kin so I can deliver your remains."

Josh stepped around the building, unsure of the reception he'd receive but not wanting to voice any of his own doubts.

Big John was standing upright, the blanket around his massive shoulders barely reaching around him against the morning chill. The plate from the night before was clean, the empty bottle on top of it.

"Good morning," greeted Josh. "I won't ask if you slept well, but I don't see any dead rattlesnakes laying around, so you must not have had to wrestle any of them. Are you hungry?"

Big John started to snarl a reply but a long look from Josh seemed to get his attention. In a less belligerent tone he said, "Man, I can eat six times a day and still be hungry. Can I have the plate of biscuits, or are you fixin' to torment me?"

"No, no, I was just testing to see what kind of mood you were in. Here you go," Josh stepped directly up to Daniels and extended the breakfast.

Big John looked down at the food, then at Josh standing less than three feet away, then at his shackled hands. He shrugged, and reached for the plate.

"You're welcome," said Josh meaningfully.

"Right—yeah, thanks," Big John mumbled.

"Nothing to it," said Josh. "I came early today so I could rig a little tarp for you before I go to smithing. I figure today's gonna be a scorcher."

"I can't understand how that second pump could have broken down so quickly." Morris was speaking to the men assembled in his office.

Dub Taylor squirmed uneasily in his chair, and looked around at the others to see if anyone else would offer an opinion. When none did, he cleared his throat roughly and began. "It sanded up real bad, I guess, and when it froze up, nobody caught it in time. The shaft is bent all to thunder. Even Josh Roberts says he can't straighten it to where it'll run true."

"How did it happen that no one was watching more closely?"

Again there was some shuffling of feet and spitting of tobacco juice into spittoons before Taylor continued. "Near as we can figure, it happened on the change of shift. Beldad's crew was comin' off, and Parker's hadn't moved in yet. Beldad here thought I was sending someone down to watch it and I thought he had detailed off somebody to stay with it." Taylor looked miserable, Beldad defiant, and Parker and the other foreman, Sexton, concerned.

"Well, this really tears it. I don't have to tell you men how far off the pace we are now. The only thing to do is abandon five for the time being. It'll take probably two weeks to replace that pump. We'll press ahead on three and hope we get a break soon."

Parker finally spoke up. "Are you gonna keep us at full crews, Mr. Morris? And if so, what'll you want the boys to be doing?"

Morris looked unhappy and stared at his desk blotter before replying. "There's no way we can absorb the expense of keeping a full roster now. Only a few at a time can work on three, the others will be laid off." There was a low murmur at this news, but no one spoke.

"Emphasize to the men that the situation is only temporary, and will be corrected as soon as five is workable again, or as soon as we make the breakthrough on three."

Sexton, the evening tower foreman, spoke up. "How'll we pick who goes and who stays? Can I keep my best men?"

Morris's reply was firm. "No. I feel an obligation to this town and those who are raising families here. We'll keep the married men and let the singles go. A man without dependents can move more easily to another job—or town, for that matter. I don't want to impose that on wives and children if I can help it."

"The men won't like that, Mr. Morris," Beldad interrupted. "It isn't fair unless it's by experience or time in the Rim. We're liable to have more trouble."

"Trouble? What sort of trouble?"

"Well, I can't say exactly, but we don't need any kind of problem with the men right now, do we?"

"I'm sorry, Mr. Beldad, but my mind's made up. I *will* support families first. We'll just have to bring the rest back as soon as we can."

———

Four nails dangled from Joshua's lips as he hefted the rear hoof of Pick's little pack mule.

"'Bout done?" Pick asked as he leaned against the door jamb of the blacksmith shop and gazed down at the forlorn figure of the prisoner.

"Hmm-mm. You in a hurry to get somewhere?" Josh muttered through the nails.

"Yup." Pick scratched his beard thoughtfully. "I aim t' be on the other side of the Sierras when you get around to unchainin' Big John." He grinned broadly, showing his nearly toothless gums, and turned to pat the mule on her rump. "Ain't that right, darlin'? We saved this here fool so's he could catch hisself a grizzly and get hisself killed proper!"

Joshua tapped in another nail and crimped the sharp point, bending it down on the outside of the hoof wall. Every nail entered the hoof at the proper angle—deep enough to hold the shoe securely, but not deep enough to nick the tender quick. It was a good job. Joshua picked up the rasp and carefully filed the rough edges of the hoof until the iron shoe blended perfectly with it. He deliberately ignored Pick's jibe.

The old prospector leaned against his mule and tried again. "I ain't but half-way jokin', boy," he sniffed. "I reckon the minute you turn Big John loose and turn your back he's gonna get hisself another gallon of ol' tangle-leg and drop an anvil on your head when you ain't lookin'."

"Then he'll find himself hugging another iron rail when he comes to, won't he?" Joshua let go of the mule's stout leg and straightened slowly.

"He can be a mean'un."

"When he's drunk."

"When he's sober, too." Pick narrowed his eyes in warning. "I reckon he's sittin' down there right now lis-tenin' to you clangin' around here in his territory, an' he's figgerin' jest what it'll take to make you git!"

Josh retrieved his tools and shrugged as the mule stretched her neck and bared her teeth, braying loudly.

"That's right, darlin'!" Pick nodded agreement. "You tell 'im! He's a durn fool if he—"

The mule's bray was answered by the whinny of a horse from the road below the shop. Pick peered out the door and in an instant forgot what he wanted to say.

"What in tarnation!" he exclaimed, stalking out of the building and raising his hand to shield his eyes against the sun.

Josh wiped his hands on his farrier chaps and fol-lowed. Behind them the mule brayed again and was an-swered by a dappled gray mare pulling a buggy. An an-cient Chinaman, complete with pigtail and black silk cap, was driving the buggy. In the seat behind him sat a young, dark-haired woman in her early twenties. Even from this distance, Joshua could see that she was lovely. *Elegant* was a better word. She wore a blue dress and carried a parasol to shield her fair skin against the sun. She sat slightly forward in her seat, and her head was tilted upward as if searching the sky for something. Her eyes were hidden by round, smoked glasses. To Joshua she looked like the very picture of the fancy ladies who rode in their carriages through the city park back home. The Chinaman driver and the bleak surroundings of the Silver Rim did not do her justice.

"Who is she?" he asked as the muttering of Pick broke into a full-scale tirade.

"Why, that good-for-nothin'. . . ! That old laundry-totin' prune of a Chinnee! I told him not t' bring her up here! Her pa is gonna hang him up by that pigtail of his!"

Josh laughed involuntarily at the image spun by Pick. It would be easy enough to hoist the tiny Chinese driver by his long gray braid. The man was not more than five feet tall and probably weighed less than a hundred pounds.

As the horse trotted smartly up the road, Josh took Pick by the arm and held him back for a moment. "Well, who are they, for goodness sake?" he demanded again.

"The one drivin' the rig—the little shriveled-up one with the droopy whiskers and the funny silk shirt—his name is Ling Duc Chow. Lean Duck, we call him around here. He's Chinnee . . ."

"I guessed that much." Joshua's eyes were riveted on the young woman.

"Says he's the oldest human on earth! An' by gum, he just about makes a feller believe it! He looks at you with them Chinnee eyes and slaps your hand like you was a kid, when all you was doin' was tryin' t' taste one o' his biscuits! Why, he told Mr. Morris I was stealin'!" Pick looked like a rooster scratching the ground before a fight. "An' now look at him, bringin' Miss Callie right up here, when I said to Mr. Morris that she ought not come!"

"Pick!" Josh spun him around in frustration. "You're not making sense!"

"Oh yes, I am! That Chinnee might a' been cookin' for Mister Morris a hunnert years longer than I been prospectin', but this time he's gone too far!"

"Pick!"

"Bringin' Miss Callie up here to feed the grizzly bear! She told me she was gonna bring supper, an' I told her—"

"Who is she?"

"Are you blind, boy?" Pick gestured angrily as the buggy pulled to a stop near the makeshift prison where Big John sat scowling toward Joshua. "That is *Miss Callie Morris!*"

"The wife of Mister—?"

"Miss! Are you deaf? His *daughter.* Head of the Temperance Union, Lord help us all! She's got no business comin' up here. It ain't no act of mercy, neither. Pure foolishness! That Lean Duck oughta be. . . ." Pick's words degenerated into an unintelligible mumble as the Chinaman tied off the reins and hurried to take the outstretched hand of the young woman. Her chin was still slightly upward, and she seemed to grope for the little man's hand.

"It ain't proper, I told her!" Pick continued. "It ain't right for a blind girl to be feedin' a black man like that!"

Blind!

Ling Duc Chow helped the lady from the buggy. She was several inches taller than he, slender and well-chproportioned. As the driver retrieved a large basket from the buggy, she waited with her hand poised expectantly. She smiled as her guide took her arm and led her over the uneven ground toward the iron rail.

Ignoring the prating of Pickax, Joshua found himself moving swiftly down the hill toward the rail and Big John. Two dozen miners, just off their shift, also gathered just beyond the perimeter of the tarp and out of sight of Big John. Pickax scurried indignantly after Joshua. Now voices and laughter floated up.

"Miss Callie!" called a dirty-faced miner. "What do you want to waste all that good food on Big John Daniels for?"

" 'Specially since he seems to want to bust up your Daddy's blacksmith shop so bad?" said another voice.

She laughed upward at the sky. "Is that Mr. Crawford there?"

"Uh . . ." He would just as soon not be identified in front of Big John.

"Well, if you remember your Bible," Miss Callie continued, "you'll recall that we are told by our Lord to feed the hungry!" She raised her voice a bit over the laughter of the spectators. "Are you hungry, Mr. Daniels?"

More laughter. Big John Daniels squirmed at the rail. A hulk that enormous was in need of vast amounts of food. Certainly a few biscuits were not enough. He lowered his chin. "Yes, ma'am. I is very hungry."

"Why don't you throw us some of that 'stead of wastin' it on a drunken black man," scowled a young miner. Someone nudged him when the young woman stopped in her tracks and snapped her head in the direction of the comment.

"God has seen to it that you are all black to me," she replied, anger in her voice. Ling Duc Chow looked first at her, then at the men, and finally at Big John. The laughter stopped abruptly. Seconds ticked past. "Now go home to your own suppers," Callie Morris said.

Joshua watched the stand-off with admiration. Here was a display of the iron-toughness the Cornish miner had warned Joshua about.

One by one the men backed up a step, tipped their hats to the sightless daughter of their boss, and left. Only Joshua and Pick silently remained at a distance. Joshua kept his fingers securely clamped around the old prospector's forearm, warning him not to interfere.

Big John sat with his back to Joshua and Pick. Callie and Ling Chow faced him. The withered little Chinaman looked directly at Joshua, but he did not mention their presence to the young woman who now took one step closer to the iron rail.

"Are they gone?" she asked quietly.

Ling Chow met Joshua's gaze again. "Yes. They are gone."

"Good," she answered. "We aren't here for a show. Where is it?" She extended her hand and Ling Chow guided it to the rail. She touched it gingerly and winced. "Horrible. Horrible to be put on display like this."

Joshua recoiled. *What else could he have done with Big John?* he thought.

"But you deserve it, Mr. Daniels," Callie continued.

"Yes'm."

"You have brought yourself to this shame."

"Yes'm."

"You were a free man, and you brought yourself back into slavery to the bottle. That's worse than being chained to this post."

"Yes'm."

"Whiskey. Who-Hit-John, they call it. Now look at you, John Daniels! Somebody hit you. Somebody bigger than you. . ."

Josh smiled slightly. Actually, Big John was a lot bigger than he.

"And I'll tell you who it was that hit you," Callie finished. "It was the *Lord!* Brought you right here in the dust. They call your whiskey *old tangle-legs*. Now look at you. Your legs all tangled around this iron rail. And you deserve everything you got because you gave up your freedom. Gave up a fine job. You did not drink like this when you shod the horses of General Grant. And now look at you!" She raised her chin. "I don't have to see you. I can *smell* you—smell the stale whiskey. You should be ashamed!"

The shiny bald head of the prisoner sagged in remorse. "That I am, Miss Callie," his voice small and sounding genuinely penitent.

Pickax jerked his head back in unbelief at the words. He stared in wonder at the bald dome and scowled when Ling Chow shrugged at him.

"I was told not to come to visit you—you, who cared well for my father's horses for so many years—but I had to see for myself. Yes, I said *see*. My soul can see quite clearly, you know, Mr. Daniels. And the Lord has told us to visit those who are in prison. He is not speaking always of walls and bars or iron rails in the ground. Sin is the prison you have chosen for yourself." The words were still direct, but her tone was compassionate.

The big man sagged in misery against the rail. "Yes, Miss Callie. Lord help me!"

"Ling Chow will feed you now," she said in a matter-of-fact voice. Then she turned to the Chinese cook. "Big John has some praying to do, Ling Chow. I shall wait in the buggy while you pray with him. Some things are not for a lady to meddle in." She turned slightly. "Read the Scriptures with him, man-to-man, when he has eaten."

Big John was weeping in earnest now. Ling Chow escorted Callie back to the buggy and helped her in. With that, the pint-sized Chinaman retrieved a small wooden stool from the buggy and placed it beside the shackled giant. He removed a well-worn Bible from the food basket, handed a plate to Big John, and filled it with food. Before he could take his first bite, Ling Chow placed a restraining hand on his arm. "Thankee God for food," he suggested, and Big John meekly bowed his head. "All good things come from your hand. We thankee you."

With that Ling Chow opened the Bible to the sixth chapter of the book of Romans, and began to read. Big John continued to nod and clank his shackles as he cried, "Amen! Yes, Lord," between bites.

Joshua and Pickax exchanged wondering looks as they retreated back to the safety of the blacksmith shop to watch the strange spectacle out of earshot. They were even more amazed to watch Big John stop eating and bury his face in his hands.

———

Pickax's amazement mellowed into a philosophical amusement after a few minutes' observation.

"Yep, my ol' ma used t' say that when a feller wakes up feelin' half-ways between 'Oh Lord,' and 'My God,' he knows he overdid it!"

"Looks to me like Miss Morris and the Chinaman

have moved Big John closer to '*Oh Lord,*' " Joshua commented dryly.

"Shoot, yeah. That pig-tailed Temperance man learned the Good Book from them Boston missionaries in the Sandwich Islands! He come as a coolie workin' the sugarcane fields." Pick spit a stream of tobacco into a ground-squirrel hole and wiped his mouth on his sleeve. "Then he come to 'Frisco on a sailin' packet in '48. Worked on the railroad as a cook for the coolie crews. Did more preachin' than cookin'. Don't ask him about it. He'll tell you more'n you want to know!"

Joshua was not as interested in Ling Chow as he was in the young woman who waited quietly beneath her parasol in the buggy. He let his gaze shift to her and linger there. Beautiful. Strong-willed. "What's a woman like her doing in Garson?" he asked Pick.

"Her pa's here. And she says one place looks the same as another to her. Since her ma passed on, she figgers her pa needs her, this bein' his last chance at makin' the Silver Rim pay off."

Joshua did not take his eyes off the slender figure. She shifted the parasol, leaving her face in shadow while the sun glinted on her thick black hair. "But she's blind. How can she be of help to Mister Morris?"

"She can't play poker or checkers, that's true enough. But she's smarter'n ten men put together. She ain't always been blind, neither. Some quack doctor put a poultice on her eyes when she was a young'un. She remembers colors and critters and just 'bout everything, I reckon. And in a way, she sees a whole lot better'n folks with two good eyes. She was one of them Christian Temperence workers in Boston, and a teacher at a blind school." Pick nodded with authority. "Yep. Readin' little bumps on paper with her fingers. She showed me—like readin' a map in the dark, I figger. 'Course I can't read a-tall, and you know I got the eyes of a brush wolf . . . spot silver from ten miles off!"

Joshua viewed the girl in the buggy with a mixture of curiosity and respect. He turned back to his work with a half-smile and the comment, "Strong woman." Retrieving a cherry-red metal bar from the fire, he placed it on the anvil for shaping beneath his hammer. He could not help but wonder about the fires and the hammer which had shaped the life of Callie Morris.

————————

Beldad addressed the group of miners assembled in the Chinaman's Chance Saloon. "It's not right, I tell you. It's not fair. Some of us been bustin' our hump longer'n anyone else for the Silver Rim, and now his highness, King Morris, up and decides to play favorites."

"Yeah," a voice responded. "You tell 'em, Beldad."

"He can't run us off."

"We'll show him he can't work the Rim without us!"

"It won't even come to that. He ain't man enough to look us in the face and tell us we ain't wanted!"

Jan Svenson, a burly Swede who normally preferred to listen rather than talk, now spoke up. "Yust a minute, Mr. Beldad. How can you be shoor Mr. Morris goin' to lay anybody off?"

"Haven't you been listenin', Swede? I'm a foreman. I tell you, I was there when Morris up and said so. He said, 'We'll send the single fellows packing—there aren't any of them worth a plugged nickle, and they're drunk all the time besides.' "

"What? That no-good polecat!" someone burst out.

"An' what about you, Mr. Beldad?" Svenson interjected. "If you are such an important fella, you must not be worried about your job. Why are you tellin' us all this?"

"Because I'm on your side, man. I aim to see everybody treated fair and square," responded Beldad.

"What'll we do, Beldad? What's the plan?"

Jan Svenson stood up, and his massive size called for respect even if his opinions didn't. "I say you are all about to give Mr. Morris a good reason to let you all go. He's been fair and straight with us all along. If I had a family here to care for, I'd be glad he gave that some weight. Besides, as long as I've got these," he declared, raising two fists the size of hams, "I can find work. After all, I was looking for a job when I found this one. Don't cross Morris, men, he's played fair with us."

Beldad glared down at the Swede, but it was a short angle even from where Beldad stood on the tabletop. Svenson looked directly back into his eyes without wavering.

Finally Beldad spoke. "Swede, there ain't no more pleasure in your company than in a wet dog's. Why don't you go on and shine old Morris's boots?"

Svenson scowled at Beldad for a moment, then spun on his heel and exited the saloon.

As he went, Beldad caught the eye of Mike Drackett, who had been standing in the shadows at the back of the meeting. As he did so, he gave Drackett the smallest of nods, and Drackett went out just after Svenson.

———

Joshua worked silently while Pick watched out the door of the smithy and muttered to himself. After a time he exclaimed, "Well, sure as my name is Pickax you're in for somethin' now!"

Joshua continued to shape glowing metal into a horseshoe without reply. He had learned that sooner or later Pickax would explain himself.

"My pa always said you could tell what a mule was thinkin' by watchin' the way his ears pointed. Now, I'll tell you—Miss Callie's got them little ears of hers pointed right up here where you're bangin' and clangin'! I bet my last nugget she's fixin' to come up here with that Lean Duck."

The thought of meeting Callie Morris pleased Joshua. Here might be opportunity to at least satisfy some of his curiosity. He imagined that she might have a word of congratulations for him since he was the only man in town who had been able to stop the rampage of Big John.

"I told you, boy! Here they come! Right up the path like they was out for a Sunday promenade in 'Frisco! It'll give me a chance t' give that Chinnee a piece of my mind! Bringin' Miss Callie out here t' feed that grizzly—"

Pick paused. "She ain't lookin' none too pleased, neither! I seen that stubborn look on her face afore, an' I know—"

Now Joshua laughed as the brash courage of Pickax seemed to fade away the closer the two came. "My daddy said, 'What you can't duck, welcome.' You afraid of a lady?" he asked, poking yet another iron in the fire and pumping the big bellows a few times. But Pick didn't reply.

Joshua was smiling when Callie Morris entered the shop with Ling Chow. His smile, like the bravado of Pickax, soon disappeared.

"Your name is Joshua Roberts, I am told?" she said,

her pretty features set with indignation.

Joshua cleared his throat. Her face turned toward him as if she were staring at him. "Yes, ma'am," he answered with respect. "And your name—"

"Callie Morris. And this is Ling Chow." She paused. "And I can tell Pickax is in the room as well. What are you doing here?"

Pickax shuffled forward, now completely docile. "Why, Miss Callie, I was jest here gettin' shoes for Jenny." He glared at Ling Chow. "Me and Josh saw that you brung supper to that ornery grizzly down there, and I was just sayin' I'll bet your pa wouldn't like you mixin' with that no-good—"

Callie raised her hand to silence his protest. "You know Big John has been a faithful employee of my father's for many years." Her tone invited no argument. "He's been trussed up like some sort of animal."

"Hold on just a minute, Miss Morris—" Josh argued.

But before he could continue she inclined her head. "No, *you* hold on. Perhaps Big John Daniels fell into bad ways, but he is not a steer to be bound hand and foot for branding."

"But Miss Callie!" Pick protested. "You ain't never seen such a mean drunk!"

"He is sober now," she said. "He needs to be released."

"I can't do that." Joshua narrowed his eyes. "Not until I'm sure—"

"I will speak to my father," Callie replied evenly, as if the matter was already settled. "In the meantime, please put up a tent for Big John."

"I did put up a tarp," Josh defended.

"Over his head." She raised her chin slightly, and her voice trembled. "But what about his—his personal, pri-

vate needs? No human should be put up to public ridi-
cule."

"Ain't nobody laughin' at Big John to his face," Pick
said quickly. "Only a fool would laugh at him out loud."

She was adamant. "He needs privacy. Even in jail,
there is some privacy. It doesn't matter what he has
done."

Joshua now regretted his curiosity. He looked at the
stack of cold iron shoes and then at Callie Morris. She
was, indeed, strong. Strong-minded. Strong-willed. Too
strong, to his way of thinking. "Ma'am, he has not been
sober for weeks. You know that as well as I know it, and
I am a newcomer here. I have done only what I needed
to do in order to restrain him."

Her face softened just a bit. "Well, that may be so.
But he does need a tent. Provide him with a chamber
pot, and water with which to wash. In private. Away
from the eyes of the miners, Mister Roberts. That is only
common decency."

She was right; Josh hadn't thought of it. He did not
like being ordered around by a woman, but she spoke
the truth. He stared at her for a moment, considering
how strange it was that a woman who could not see was
so aware of what it meant for Big John to be totally
without privacy.

"Yes, Miss Morris," Josh replied. "Common decency."

"Thank you," she said abruptly, turning to reach for
Ling Chow's arm. "We are agreed," she continued. "Ling
Chow and I will be back with breakfast for him in the
morning. I hope this matter will be taken care of before
then." Her tone indicated that Josh probably wouldn't
want to be around if she found anything different than
that.

Josh and Pickax exchanged looks as Callie Morris and Ling Chow drove away from the blacksmith shop.

"Well, Pick," Josh said dryly, "I purely admire the way you gave them a piece of your mind."

CHAPTER 6

Joshua awoke early, for a moment not certain what had interrupted his peaceful sleep. He lay on his cot, glancing out the window toward where the faintest of predawn gray was beginning to brighten the eastern sky. He looked around the packed room; none of the miners were awake. Listening to the chorus of snores, snorts, and wheezes, Josh couldn't imagine that any outside sound had penetrated even these thin walls.

Then he heard it again: the call of a horse, answered by another, and the clattering of hoofs on the rocky slope leading upward toward Garson from the desert below. Josh swung his legs over the cot and sat up, drawing on his Levis and thrusting his stockinged feet into his boots.

Joshua clumped downstairs. On the way he heard the banging of pans in the kitchen, indicating that Mrs. Flynn was getting the day in order, but he saw no one.

Out to the board sidewalk he went, leaned over a rail, and looked down the slope. Now he could hear human voices mixed in with the horse whinnies. One said, "Get up there," and another called, "Whoop, whoop." A couple of sharp whistles and the sound of a coiled rope smacking against a leather-covered thigh accompanied the voices.

Presently the first of the herd of horses came into

view. They were scruffy, wild-looking creatures, with flaring nostrils and tangled manes and tails.

A rider galloped up alongside the herd to unlatch and open the corral gate. He did this all from the back of his horse, a beautiful glossy-coated bay. At a slight urging from the reins, the horse backed up to block the road.

The rider then removed his hat and stood in his stirrups to wave the leading horses into the pen. As he did so, Josh got a good look at this tall man who rode with such assurance. He was flamboyantly dressed in a bright yellow shirt with a bright red bandana knotted at his throat. But the most amazing aspect was the man himself: he was black.

The herd of wild horses needed little urging from the black cowboy. As they came within sight of the corral, they could smell the watering trough, and into the gate they turned.

A second cowboy had come up along the left side of the herd. He was white, similar in size to the first rider, equal in horsemanship as well as age. Both men looked to be in their early twenties.

Josh counted fifteen horses as they paced into the corral. The black horseman moved his bay back up to the gate and shut it quickly behind the last mustang. The drag rider was older than the other two and had a slightly shorter and stockier build. His sun-browned face broke into an easy grin as he slapped the back of first one cowboy and then the other in mutual congratulations.

Josh strolled down toward the pen, curious about the obviously friendly group. As he approached, the three were just dismounting and preparing to lead their horses into the livery stable.

"Howdy." The older rider spoke to Josh as he passed by into the barn. The other two touched their hat brims and nodded politely, but said nothing.

Josh could overhear the instructions the older man gave the livery man regarding the care and feeding of the saddle horses and the rough stock. "Grain these three up good. We had planned to be here last night but ran out of daylight up the trail apiece, so we turned 'em into a box canyon an' come in this morning."

The three riders strode back out into the brightening morning light. Garson was beginning to come to life, and the sounds of the awakening town filled the air.

"Wonder where's a good place to put on *our* feed bag, Pa?"

"I don't know, Nate, but perhaps this gentleman can tell us," the older man said as he approached Joshua.

"Yes, sir," replied Josh politely. "I think you'd find the food at my hotel, the Tulare, to your liking. Mrs. Flynn's cooking isn't fancy, but she doesn't stint on the portions."

"Sounds just like what we need, eh, boys?"

"You bet," the younger white man responded.

The black cowboy replied, "Sounds good to me, Pa," to Josh's surprise.

"Lead the way, young man," said the man to Josh. "And perhaps you'll join us and give us some information about this town."

The introductions which followed Josh's agreement revealed that the older man was Tom Dawson, a rancher from Greenville on the other side of the Sierras. "Up in God's country," Dawson said, "where the land grows grass and trees instead of rocks and cactus."

Tom gestured to the younger white man and indicated him to be his nephew, Nathan. He referred to the black cowboy as his son, Mont James.

Mrs. Flynn was pleased to have three more paying customers for breakfast, and when Tom indicated that they were interested in a room as well, she was even more generous in ladling out gravy for their biscuits.

"What brings you to Garson, Mr. Dawson?" inquired Josh.

"We've been rounding up wild stock out of the desert and breaking them for the army," Tom replied. "But the army's interests of late have moved quite far from California, what with the Sioux troubles and all, so our market's dried up some. Anyway, Mont here had an idea. Tell him, Mont."

The black cowboy finished swallowing a mouthful of biscuit and washed it down with a quick swig of coffee before answering. "I thought maybe we could find some takers in these mining towns who were in need of desert-bred stock. Plus I figured if we rounded them up and did the breaking here, instead of driving them home and back again, it'd save some expense and wear and tear on us."

"Anyway," broke in the one named Nathan, "we thought we'd make this a trial run and see how it turns out. Would you be interested in purchasing a fine broke horse, Mr. Roberts?"

"I don't think I can afford one just yet. And I should tell you that I'm probably not the one to ask for information about Garson. You see, I'm pretty new here myself."

"You didn't steer us wrong about the food," said Tom. "Why don't you just fill us in on what you do know?"

Josh described the town's situation as best he could, including the troubles besetting the Silver Rim and Mr.

Morris's efforts to make it pay. "I don't know that you'll find many buyers among the mine workers. They don't have anywhere to go and not much money to spend. But the storekeepers and merchants sure might be interested."

"I guess we'll sound them out directly," concluded Tom. "Anyway, we plan to put up here for a month or so while we're putting some school on these cayuses."

Chief Pitahaya regarded the two young Mojave Indians before him. *Sotol and Turtleback have shown some courage,* he thought. *Perhaps their smoldering hatred of the whites can be fanned into flame.*

"Sotol," Pitahaya said to the taller and brighter of the two, "have you had any word of Yellow Plume since she ran away with the white man?"

Through gritted teeth Sotol replied, "As you know, Pitahaya, her brother here and I tracked them to the white village of Dar-win. But the whites there laughed at our demand that she be returned."

"Indeed," Turtleback added. "They called us *dirty Injun* and drove us out of their village with rocks."

Pitahaya eyed them both. "How is it that you let such insults stand, my brothers?"

Sotol and Turtleback exchanged looks. Sotol replied, "They have guns with which to give their taunts force, Pitahaya. Pistols and long-guns which shoot many times, while we have none."

"So," mused Pitahaya thoughtfully, "you do not lack courage, only guns. Is that so?"

At the nods of the two younger men, he continued, "Here is what should be done. In the white village of

Gar-son they sell the guns which shoot many times—"
Pitahaya raised his hand to cut off the protest he saw
coming. "What we must seek are the whites who newly
come to this land and who would not be sought after
should they lose their way in our desert. Do you understand?"

Sotol and Turtleback grunted in reply. They agreed
to take turns watching Garson, exchanging places from
Wild Rose Canyon by night.

―――――――

"Good day, Mr. Jacobson," called Callie to the proprietor as she left the hardware store.

"Yah. Und tank-you, Miss Morris," replied the portly
little shopkeeper.

Callie felt the stares of two men she had heard enter
the store after her. *They must be new in town,* she thought.

"Und what can I do mit you, gentlemen?" Jacobson
asked.

Their full reply was cut off by the closing door, but
not before Callie heard, *"Do you have ammunition for
Winchester . . ."*

―――――――

"Come along, Ling Chow, don't dawdle," chided Callie Morris over her shoulder.

"No, Missie, I comin' plenty fast," puffed the little
Chinaman over the basket he carried piled high with
groceries.

Callie strode briskly along the boardwalk in front of
Jacobson's Hardware Store. Her familiarity with the
limited business district of Garson enabled her to walk
with all the assurance of a sighted person.

She paused when her hand encountered the gap in the rail indicating the front of Fancy Dan's Saloon. Here she turned and prepared to cross the road to her carriage, which was tied up in front of her father's office.

Callie listened carefully for a moment, preferring to judge for herself if the street was clear for crossing rather than calling on Ling Chow's assistance.

While she waited, a carefully modulated voice spoke from behind her. "Good day to you, Miss Morris. May I offer you my arm in crossing the street?"

Callie recognized Dan McGinty's voice and replied, "No, thank you, Mr. McGinty, I can manage just fine."

"But I insist," he said, stepping up in a flourish of brocade vest, and what was to Callie a wave of bay rum. He gently but firmly placed her left hand on his right arm and prepared to step out across the street.

"May I say how lovely you look this morning, Miss Morris? You certainly add a note of classic beauty to our humble surroundings."

"You are a flatterer, Mr. McGinty, and a rather forward one at that," Callie responded tartly, lifting her hand from his forearm.

"If I cannot be of service, then I certainly don't wish to impose," said McGinty, with a quick fan of breeze that indicated a sweeping bow. Then he was gone with a light step and a creak of new leather boots.

Callie paused a moment, her cheeks burning. *I must like his flattery a bit*, she admitted to herself. *But he is not a man I can trust*, she thought as she walked determinedly to her carriage.

———

"And you are certain, Sotol, that these two white men

know no one in the white village on the rocky slopes?"

"No one, Pitahaya. I was outside the Place of Iron Tools when I saw them leave and heard them ask directions of the prospector known as Pickax.

"The man pointed them toward the north and told them of water to be found at such and such a place. Then they told that they were from the land of the Utes and were newly come to this place."

"We think," said Turtleback, "that the meaning is clear: they are so newly come as to need directions to water. When they obtained food, they left again quickly without being much regarded."

Pitahaya nodded slowly. "And what have they of use to us?"

Sotol glanced at Turtleback before replying. "That is truly the best part, Pitahaya. Each carries a shining Colt six-shooter and a Yellow Belly. We saw them load boxes of bullets for these on their two fine, strong horses."

"You have done well, Sotol, and you also, Turtleback. Now, let us plan what is to be done. Will they camp near Three Kill Spring tomorrow night?"

"Yes, Pitahaya. We believe we can meet up with them in the canyon that lies before Three Kill Spring."

CHAPTER 7

"Hey, somebody better come here, quick!"

"What's the matter, what is it?"

"I dunno—is somebody snakebit?"

"Could be—I just heard the hollerin'."

There was a flurry of activity around the first dry wash north of Garson. Someone had spotted something at the bottom of the little canyon and gone down to investigate. Immediately afterward came a series of yells until a stream of miners had scrambled down the rocky slope, around the jutting overhang of rock, and into the bottom of the draw.

"It's Swede Svenson!"

"Sure enough is. Is he hurt?"

"I'll say so! He's dead!"

"Dead? What happened to him?"

"Don't be thick! Look up there at that drop and then where he's layin'. He musta got drunk and walked off that cliff in the night and broke his fool neck."

"Powerful shame. I liked ol' Swede—he was a good'n. And I never knew him to be much on drinkin'. But he'd have to be drunk to end up down here."

The lead horse, a tall, long-necked bay, pricked his

ears forward again. His rider took no notice and neither did his partner, riding a few paces behind and leading a pack animal.

But the second rider's horse, a smaller and better-proportioned, apron-faced sorrel did catch some of the other horse's agitation. Neither horse stopped, shied, or snorted an alarm, however, and the riders were too inexperienced to catch the subtle signs.

The canyon through which they were riding was narrow and winding, the sandstone walls rising thirty to forty feet on either side. Yucca and creosote bushes grew on the plateaus, but the canyon walls and floor were almost without vegetation. A blue-bellied lizard skittered out from between the lead horse's feet and disappeared into a crack in a low ledge.

The two men knew where they were headed, but not how long it would take them. Their destination was Three Kill Spring, where they had been told they would find water.

Both men suffered from the worst malady that could befall a desert traveler—overconfidence. Even though both men realized that they were new to the desert and its ways, neither was smart enough to feel the least apprehensive or even cautious.

The two young men, easterners out for an adventure, had come west intending to prospect for silver and gold in the Comstock Lode. When they reached the Great Salt Lake, they met up with a returning party of discouraged prospectors. They were told all that was left was hard work for poor pay.

The two were considering going straight on to San Francisco before returning east by ship when they heard some interesting news. Silver had been located in the

Panamint Range and the Argus Range of eastern California. They began to hear names like Death Valley, Lone Pine and Darwin.

By train they got as far as Carson City, Nevada, then turned south and took the stage for Independence, California. At Independence they parted with some of their stake and proceeded to outfit themselves.

They bought horses, packs, mess kits, and boots, picks and shovels, flour and coffee. Most exciting of all to their spirit of adventure were their firearms—brand-new, six-shot Colt revolvers and lever-action Winchester rifles nicknamed "Yellow Bellies" because their brass receivers gleamed golden yellow in the light.

Their choice of weapons happened to be a good one; both pistol and rifle fired the same .44 caliber ammunition, making it unnecessary to carry two different loads. Unfortunately, neither knew how to hit anything that wasn't stationary, and neither had ever had occasion to fire a shot in self-defense.

The man on the lead horse turned in his saddle to inspect his companion's progress. "That pack saddle is slipping again, William."

William also turned around and regarded the mound of gear loaded on the last animal. The canvas-covered bundle of supplies was leaning precariously to the left. In their travels so far, the supplies had never been carried for more than two hours without a stop to readjust and tighten the ropes.

Their concern about the pack was caused by an experience they'd had early after leaving Independence. After a lengthy spell of inattention, the gear had slipped completely under the pack horse, and the lead rope had come loose. Two miles later they finally caught up with the horse, but it took another half day to recover all their belongings, strewn over a thousand acres of sagebrush, granite boulders, and ground squirrel holes. They never did find the package of chewing tobacco, but neither of them chewed, so it wasn't much loss. They had only bought the tobacco on the advice of the storekeeper, who told them that all salty prospectors chewed.

"You're right, Lawrence. I suppose we'd better stop and fix it right now." William pulled his red horse to a stop.

He struggled with the girth that secured the pack frame. When he first tried to right the load by yanking on the offside, it refused to budge. He loosened the cinch that secured the pack frame, but it began to slip before he got around the animal again. He returned to stop its slide and succeeded in pushing it back upright, but the ineptly tied load had shifted under the canvas and so continued to lean.

Frustrated, William looked up at his partner who, still mounted, was staring intently up the canyon. In an exasperated tone William said, "Aren't you going to help me, Lawrence?"

Lawrence gestured for silence without turning around, and as his angry partner moved up beside him, he said in a hoarse whisper, "Did you see him?"

"See him? Him who?"

"An Indian, I think. I didn't see anyone when we were riding or when we stopped, except just out of the corner of my eye. I thought I saw someone stand up, and as I turned to face him, he disappeared."

"You're imagining things. Or perhaps it was a mirage."

"Why would a mirage suddenly appear and then disappear?"

"Who can explain what a trick of refracted light may do? Come on, give me a hand with this pack animal, or we'll never make the spring by nightfall."

Lawrence stood up in his stirrups and surveyed the trail ahead before shaking his head and stepping down from the animal.

Together the men spent twenty minutes untying, rearranging, and re-securing their belongings. The load looked no more secure than before, but at least it perched mostly upright. Both men remounted the horses and prepared to continue forward.

"Don't you think we should at least have our weapons handy?" asked Lawrence.

"I can't think that we'll be needing them, but if it will make you feel better, all right."

Both men drew their shiny new Winchesters from leather rifle boots and chambered rounds of ammunition. Following instructions, they carefully let the hammers down to the half-cock safety positions. They were sure they were ready for any trouble.

They topped a ridge of sand in the canyon's throat, a formation that would have been an island in time of flood. Before them the canyon opened out wider on either side and the steep walls leveled out at the bottom.

"You see, Lawrence?" insisted William, "there's nothing in sight for miles. Besides, if Indians were lying in wait for us, why wouldn't they have attacked us back in the narrow part of the canyon?"

"I suppose you're right," replied Lawrence, attempting to urge the bay down the sand bank. But the horse was suddenly uncooperative. He shifted his weight from one foot to the other and swung his head from side to side, as if being asked to make a dangerous leap. His rider didn't help matters by pulling reins counter to each movement of the horse's neck until both came to a confused stop.

"What's the matter now?" called William.

"It's nothing; he's just being fractious. Come on, fellow, come on," replied Lawrence, and he administered a kick to his mount's ribcage with both heels. The bay jerked forward, blundering between two sand piles on the short slope.

Instantly the heaps of sand erupted. Sotol jumped up to grab the startled lead horse's bridle, while on the other side, another Mojave jumped to his feet and seized the .44 rifle.

A more seasoned man would have instantly given up his hold on the rifle and drawn the Colt at his side, but such experience was not available to Lawrence, and he struggled to retain the Winchester. With the horse being pulled one way and the struggle for the yellow belly taking place on the other, rider and horse parted company and Lawrence was thrown to the ground. He had only a moment to experience the pain of an arm broken underneath him in his fall, for the successful Mojave spun the captured rifle in a flashing arc that brought it smashing down on Lawrence's head. After that he felt nothing at all.

Sotol let the bay prance around in a circle as he held on to the bridle and watched the end of the tug-of-war for the rifle. Then he turned to see what had happened to the other white man.

Turtleback and a fourth Mojave had also been disguised as mounds of earth forming a line just below the rim of sand. Their simple strategy had been to arrange themselves so that Lawrence had to descend the slope between two Indians. Turtleback and his companion had also jumped up when Sotol struck, but they ran immediately toward William and the pack horse.

William's reactions were no quicker than Lawrence's, but he had a moment longer to think. He saw the struggle for possession of the rifle, and as the other two Indians ran toward him, he threw down the lead rope of the pack animal and raised the Winchester to his shoulder. By sheerest good fortune, his first shot took Turtleback in the cheek, shattering his face and taking off a considerable part of the back of his skull as it exited.

His second shot missed the other Mojave entirely, and in that same moment the Indian threw a razor-sharp hatchet that hit William just below the knee and neatly sliced down his shin bone. William cried out and almost dropped the rifle, but his horse showed greater presence of mind; the sorrel spun around to bolt back into the canyon. William saw in a whirling glimpse the descent of the rifle butt on Lawrence's head.

William reeled in the saddle and almost fell. He held both reins and rifle in his right hand as with his left he clutched his bloody leg and bent low over the horse's neck.

Through eyes almost squinted shut against the pain, he could see the pack horse racing ahead of him back the way they had come. An oddly detached part of his mind noted with chagrin that the pack had once again slipped and the supplies were being distributed over the landscape.

He had just had time to notice this when the remaining two Mojaves, who had remained hidden to cut off such an escape, jumped up to block his path. Their sudden appearance made the already panicked pack animal rear and swing broadside to the on-rushing sorrel. In the collision William went flying over both horses, the spinning rifle sparkling golden in the sunlight.

One of the Mojaves caught the Winchester in mid-air and waved it in triumph. The other rushed to stand over William, only to discover as he bent to slit the white man's throat that William's neck had snapped; he was already dead.

———————

Tom Dawson had asked Josh to see to the shoeing needs of their three mounts, and so Josh was working beside the corral after his smithing duties at the mine were done for the day.

The three cowboys were finishing their own day's efforts, sacking some horses who were still pulling back against lead ropes, putting weighted saddles on others, and tying still others up to stand with bits in their mouths.

Josh had already completed the shoeing of Tom's mount, a horse named Duncan, and was fitting a second shoe to Mont's. After clenching the nails and ringing them off, he allowed the hoof to slip to the ground and straightened up with a creak of backbones.

"Hey, Josh," called Nate Dawson, "which of these plug-uglies do you like best?"

Josh let his eyes rove over the herd standing in varying degrees of submission. All were lean and scraggly in appearance, but one caught his attention. The animal Josh admired was taller than the rest, a buckskin with a dark mane and tail and four black stockings. He stood with his head held high and his body turned along the length of the rail to which he was snubbed. He appeared to be watching the proceedings in the corral with an intelligent and interested eye.

Josh waved toward him and replied, "That buck there."

Mont looked over from the roan he was sacking and commented, "You got a good eye, Josh. I figure he ran off from somebody; he's mostly broke already. Not like this fleabag." He indicated the roan which had begun plunging and straining at the lead rope even *before* Mont had waved the saddle blanket.

"Well, I'll be hogtied and horn-swoggled!" Mont exclaimed. Josh followed the line of the black man's outstretched arm past the buckskin, beyond the corral to the mesquite-covered hillside beyond.

Down the trail slanting away from Garson rode Pickax on Jenny. Behind him, at the end of a lead rope, was a stylish gray mare, and seated on that mare was a very erect young woman wearing smoked-lens glasses.

"That is Miss Callie Morris," Josh explained, "the daughter of mine superintendent Morris. I didn't know she could ride, and I'll bet her daddy doesn't know she's doing it, either."

All four men stopped to observe the progress of the two riders across the field. Apparently Pickax was calling out instructions over his shoulder, for he kept turning in his saddle, first one way and then the other, to watch Callie's ride.

And then it happened. As he was turned to watch her, a rattlesnake must have buzzed across the path in front of them. Jenny was a desert-wise creature who didn't buck or bolt, but her sidestep and twist off the trail was enough to tumble the backward-facing Pick into the dirt.

The gray was neither desert-bred nor very bright. At

the first nervous activity by Jenny and Pick's clumsy sprawl right in front of her, the mare reared and bolted off across the hillside.

By sheer grit and determination, Callie kept her seat, but whether this was good fortune or bad remained to be seen. The mare, sensing the inability of the rider to gain control, plunged headlong through the mesquite and creosote, occasionally leaping over clumps of brush. And, of course, with every stride the horse was in danger of dropping a leg into a ground-squirrel hole or coming to grief on the uneven ground.

Josh took in the unfolding disaster at a glance. Without a second thought he threw himself at Duncan's lead rope. With a yank on the quick release that spun the startled horse around, he vaulted onto Duncan's back.

"Dear God, help Miss Callie!" came unbidden to his frantic mind as he felt the cowpony gather his haunches under him and spring away from the rail. He desperately hoped that the horse would respond to leg pressure, for he had only the free end of the lead rope in one hand and a handful of mane in the other.

Josh inmediately discovered just how well-trained Duncan was. Tom Dawson's jug-headed horse was nothing special to look at, but he was smart and quick to pick up what was needed in the situation.

Almost as if he knew without being told what Josh wanted, Duncan galloped after the bolting mare. His great muscled neck stretched out front. His ears were pricked forward, and it was obvious that he was enjoying the chase.

The same could not be said of Josh. The blood was pounding through his heart like the hammer on his anvil. His breath caught in his throat with each leap and pivot of the gray mare, and he was filled with dread for the moment when he would see Callie flying off the mare's back to be broken against the rocky slope. The thought that this uncontrolled, desperate flight was happening to a blind girl made him full of unspeakable horror and dismay.

He urged Duncan to even greater speed. For what seemed like an agonizingly long time, the gap between the racing horses remained the same, until at last Duncan's greater muscle and length of stride began to tell.

As Josh and Duncan began to overtake the mare, Josh shouted ahead to Callie, "Hold on, Miss Morris, I'll get her stopped for you."

Over her shoulder, blown to him on the wind of the rushing horses, he heard, "I—have—no—intention—of—letting—go!"

Gradually, Duncan drew up alongside the racing mare. Lathered with exertion and fear, the gray rolled a wild eye sideways at Duncan before spurting away again. A quarter of a mile ahead, Josh could see the line of mesquite shrub beginning to dip into a boulder-strewn ravine.

Josh leaned far out over the horse's right shoulder, holding with great difficulty to both lead rope and mane clutched in his left hand.

He had to trust completely in the sureness of Duncan's pace and in the horse's sense of what was at stake. He urged Duncan on to the limit.

His fingertips stretched out toward the bridle of the mare. Another inch closer, and Josh glanced over at the blind girl. Though she had not screamed, her clenched fists on the reins and her face, completely drained of color, spoke of her fear.

Now his fingers touched the bridle, grasped the cheek strap, and pulled the mare alongside Duncan as Josh straightened himself upright. Still apprehensive that the mare would pitch Callie off, he did not try to bring her to an abrupt stop. Instead, he turned Duncan and the gray in a wide circle around to the left, back toward Garson. "It's all right, Miss Morris, I've got her now. Just another moment," he assured her as calmly as he could.

Slowly slackening Duncan's speed, Josh brought the mare under control. At last Josh turned them through the deepest sand he could find, and the gray gave up the race and shuddered to a stop.

Josh slid off Duncan wrong-sided, afraid to give up his grip on the bridle. When he stood alongside the mare, he shoved his left shoulder up under the gray's chin; only then did he reach up to assist Callie Morris down from the side-saddle on which she had perched for two terrifying miles.

"Here, Miss Morris, let me help you down. It's Josh. Josh Roberts. I've got you."

"Thank you," she gasped, "oh, thank you. I'm quite all right, Mr. Roberts—" she began. Then she collapsed into his arms with her face buried against his chest, the two horses snorting off steam and pawing the sand. Josh couldn't help but notice that she smelled like wildflowers.

———

"You there! Yes, you, Indian. Come here." McGinty gestured emphatically toward Sotol, who had been squatting unobtrusively around the corner of Fancy Dan's Saloon out of view of the street.

Sotol looked up, then away, staring out at the mesquite as if he hadn't heard a word.

McGinty walked over to the Mojave and stood, eyes squinted, regarding him. "I know you speak English; I saw you look up when I first called you."

Sotol grudgingly agreed, "I speak."

"Yes, and you understand even more than you speak, curse you. Now get up, I need you to carry a message to your chief."

Sotol looked up slowly and returned McGinty's stare.

Looking into those hard dark eyes, McGinty almost changed his mind and turned to walk back into his saloon. He swung back, trying to give as much smoldering hatred to his gaze as the Indian was giving him but found himself looking away.

Angrily he reached in his vest and withdrew a .44 shell from his watch pocket. He threw it down at the Indian's feet. "Go show that to your chief. Tell him I want to talk to him about it. Tell him I'll be at the old shack by Poison Well tomorrow night at moonrise."

Sotol looked at the shell lying on the ground, but gave no indication of agreement, not even a grunt. McGinty was inwardly relieved at the break in eye contact, so he didn't press the issue. He turned around and went to the outside staircase leading to his office.

As he reached the corner of the building he glanced over his shoulder. Sotol and the cartridge were gone. Though the plain around had no brush taller than three feet for miles in all directions, the Mojave had disappeared as completely as if he'd never been there at all.

CHAPTER 8

Joshua soaped up again as Pick dumped yet another bucket of steaming water over his head.

"Somehow it just don't seem right usin' precious water for washin' all over." Pick shook his head in disapproval. He kicked the small tin bathtub where Josh sat folded up like an accordion. "And what's gonna happen to this water after you get out of it? Why, it ain't good for nuthin'. Can't cook in it. Can't drink it." He sniffed thoughtfully. "S'pose a feller could water his mule with it, 'cept the soap would make it sick."

"Well now, Pickax," Josh said as he scrubbed his neck, "we might be able to stretch the use of this water. You can take a bath after me."

"No, thanks. It ain't natural, a man gettin' wet all over. Don't know why you want to do it. Miss Callie ain't gonna see if you've got clean ears or dirty."

"No, but she has a fine-honed sense of smell. She recognized you by odor the other day in the blacksmith shop."

Pick aimed at the spittoon and let fly with a bullet of tobacco. "And I wouldn't think of deprivin' the lady o' that clue, neither. Why she's gonna think Joshua Roberts skedaddled and sent a well-oiled Mississippi gambler over to eat supper in his place. She ain't gonna know

you, all sweet smellin' like lye soap an' lavender water!
You better sleep in the livery stable tonight when you're
done, or one o' these drunk miners is likely to mistake
you for one of them Calico Queens!"

With that, Joshua dipped the tin cup into the water
and drenched the old prospector. "Take your own gol
durn bath!" Pickax roared. "Now I'm gonna smell like a
wet dog!"

"That's some improvement, anyway," Joshua howled
as Pickax hurled the bucket at him and stomped out of
the small room.

————

The truth was, Joshua had no explanation as to why
he now stood in front of the washstand mirror and
worked to straighten the part in his hair. Pick was right.
Callie Morris couldn't see him, so why had he taken a
week's earnings and spent an hour at the general store
picking out a new shirt and trousers and a celluloid collar? Why had he stood scowling down at the too short
sleeves of the only Sunday-go-to-meetin'-coat in the
place? Why had he washed his socks and dusted off his
derby hat like some city slicker greenhorn from St.
Louis?

Indeed, it was a mystery even to him. But when she
had collapsed into his arms, when she had leaned
against him, showing she was made of much softer stuff
than he had thought, he had forgotten that she could not
see him. As he had lifted her onto Duncan and escorted
her back, he'd had the fleeting thought that in the future
she should not meet him on the street and recognize him
by the same method she had identified old Pick!

She was truly a beautiful woman—as fine and mysterious and strong—yes, and soft and sweet—as any woman he had ever seen. That kind of beauty deserved to be in the company of a man with a straight part and a clean shirt. After all, she hadn't invited a mule to supper, so Joshua reasoned he ought not smell like one!

Garson had no flowers for Joshua to bring to her, so after he had bought his new duds, he spent his last two bits on a bottle of lilac water. He hadn't forgotten that her skin smelled like a flower garden. He would bring her the scent as a token of the flowers he did not have.

———

Joshua had not counted on Pickax's ability to provide an instant crowd of grimy spectators. As he emerged from the boardinghouse, a chorus of hoots and yelps and hurrahs greeted him.

A group of two dozen laughing miners swelled to four dozen as he strode, red-faced, down the street. The No-Name Saloon emptied out when customers mistook the cheering, jeering uproar for a brawl.

"Ain't never seen a blacksmith so clean!"

"Kin you *smell* him? Hey, Josh! You fall into a barrel of eau de toilette or somethin'?"

"He's either died or he's gettin' hitched!"

"What's the difference?"

"He smells too nice to be dead!"

"Naw! That's the new embalming fluid!"

"It shore beats ice!"

"So does a warmhearted woman!"

At that, Joshua stopped in the center of the street and turned around to face the audience. The last comment had pushed the fun too far. After all, Miss Callie Morris was for sure not one of the girls in the town bordello.

The men nudged each other playfully as they saw Joshua's obvious irritation. He clenched and unclenched his fists and stared down the rowdies.

The laughter died to a nervous twittering.

"Who said that?" Joshua's voice was low and menacing.

Silence fell over the crowd. *This is the man who beat Big John Daniels. This is the man who* . . .

The men gulped and stepped back, their smiles apologetic. They knew they had gone too far.

Pickax shrugged. "We didn't mean nothin' by it, Josh. The fellers wasn't talkin' about Miss Callie disrespectful. They was just meanin' that women in general was better than ice."

Josh considered his words. He scowled deep and mean at a young fella who seemed to have developed the shakes. "You think women are better than ice, do you?" Josh growled. *"Well, I say* . . . *that just depends on how hot the desert is!"*

With that the group once again roared with laughter. Grimy hands reached out to clap Joshua on the back as he yelled above the boisterous tumult, *"Now quit following me before I take you on one at a time!"*

Content, the group turned back to the saloons of Garson, leaving Joshua to walk the last quarter mile to the Morris house in peace.

———

Joshua had hoped that the invitation to dine at the Morris home had been Callie's idea. Now as she sat silently across the table from him, Josh was certain that the invitation had been Mr. Morris's plan.

The small, tissue-wrapped bottle of perfume seemed

to mock him from his pocket. *What were you thinking of, Josh Roberts? Even if she could see your face, she wouldn't look twice at you. You're a blacksmith, not a gentleman.* The new collar seemed suddenly too tight. The starch in his shirt made the fabric rustle when he reached out for the bowl of mashed potatoes. He wondered if word had gotten back to Callie that he had bought himself new duds for the occasion. He wondered if she could sense his embarrassment.

Ling Chow placed a heaping platter of fried chicken in front of Callie as Mr. Morris laid the purpose of this meeting on the table.

"I'd like to appoint you town constable, Joshua. Marshal of Garson, if you prefer that title," Morris announced as though it was already accomplished.

Joshua ducked his head slightly, and after letting the words sink in, he chuckled carefully. "I prefer blacksmith. Just . . . blacksmith, Mr. Morris."

Now it was Morris's turn to chuckle, and he glanced at Callie, who did not respond. "You were right, daughter." He turned back to Josh. "She told me you wouldn't want the job."

"She was right. I . . . I thank you, Mr. Morris, for the honor—if it is an honor. But I've no desire to get near anything hotter than my forge."

Morris stuck out his lower lip and again glanced first at Callie then back at Joshua as he considered the refusal. "You're a good man, Joshua. Good with your fists, and good with this." Morris tapped his forehead lightly. "Any fool can pack a sidearm. I could hire two dozen gunslingers tomorrow and pin badges on them, but they'd still just be trash behind tin stars. No. The Silver Rim . . . Garson . . . we're in need of a man who can think on his feet. You're our man."

"I've had little choice in any of the circumstances. It's not that I—"

"Nonsense!" Morris interrupted his protest. "If you had not done what you did, Callie would be dead. Tom Dawson said as much, and I believe him to be a man who speaks the truth."

Joshua shrugged. He had lost his appetite. The thought of keeping the peace in a town like Garson was the last assignment he wanted. "Anyone would have—"

"And then there is the matter of Big John." Morris cleared his throat authoritatively. "Not easy for you to say that anyone would have stopped *him*. But you found another way. I've been out in the West long enough to know that plenty of men have used the law as an excuse for killing. You had plenty of reason to pull the trigger and put Big John permanently into a hole in the ground. No one would have blamed you."

Callie still did not react to her father even though Josh was quite certain she would have had plenty to say if Big John Daniels had been killed. "I might have killed him," Josh admitted, "if I had thought of it." He looked quickly at Callie, trying to judge her expression.

Again Mr. Morris raised his hand to silence Joshua. "Tom Dawson tells me you were admiring that big lanky buckskin they're breaking down there." Was Morris changing the subject?

"He seemed the best of the remuda," Joshua nodded, relieved that the conversation had taken a different turn.

"He's yours, then."

"But—"

"It would not be proper for the Constable of Garson to go around on foot."

"But, Mr. Morris—"

"You'll need a saddle. Pick out something down at the livery stable and send the bill to me. Tom Dawson and those boys of his will finish breaking the buck and then choose a second horse from the herd. You might need a spare."

Joshua glared at the oblivious mine-owner. Now he could see where Callie Morris had acquired her obstinate nature. He waited until he was certain that Mr. Morris had finished speaking.

"I am just a blacksmith, Mr. Morris. Every day of my life since I was a boy, I've wrestled with horses and mules and pounded hot iron. It's no miracle that I could wrestle down John Daniels, no great shakes that I could pound him into submission. He is smaller than a horse and less ornery than a mule. There is nothing unusual in what I have done." He paused a moment, then said as firmly as he could, "I am no lawman."

Callie now smiled softly. She turned her face slightly away from him and said almost coyly. "Come now, Mr. Roberts. Some men have the law written in their hearts. My father has taken you for one of those."

Morris nodded. "That makes you lawman enough for me."

"Steel," Callie said in a voice that touched on admiration, "tempered with the gentleness of mercy." Her face shone in the soft glow of the candles in their silver candlesticks. Joshua saw his own reflection in the smoked glass of her spectacles. He felt trapped, unable to refuse her words or the tone of her voice. "My father is right, Mr. Roberts. You are quite ideal for the position."

"Except that I don't *want* it," Joshua replied incredulously.

Morris looked toward his daughter as if appealing for help. Although she could not see her father's face, she seemed to understand his feelings instinctively.

She smiled as if coaxing a reluctant child. "Joshua," she said, using his given name for the first time, "often we are called on to do things we do not wish to do. But we do them because there is simply no one else." She laid her hand palm up on the table. Instinctively, he responded to her gesture and placed his fingers against hers. It was as if their eyes had met.

"But there must be someone else," he said lamely.

"No," she replied, "there is no one else. You're the man for the job."

———

McGinty paced around inside the tumbledown shack, absently kicking a broken chair leg. Mike Drackett, who was leaning against the door frame, grinned at his boss's discomfort and remarked, "If you'd set down a spell you wouldn't be raisin' so much dust."

"Shut up!" said McGinty abruptly. "They aren't coming after all. Look there—" He gestured toward the almost-full moon which had risen over the starkly outlined cinder cone to the east. "We've been here since an hour before moonrise, and now it's an hour past. Let's get out of here; maybe this was a dumb idea all along."

Drackett was surprised to hear Fancy Dan admit to having second thoughts. *'Course, it's not like I wasn't havin' no jitters myself,* he thought, then said, "You was gonna give them Mojaves rifles to stick up the stage, is that right?"

"Certainly. Only *we'd* tell them which ones to attack

so as to cause Morris the most grief over lost payroll and people."

A sigh, softer than a breath of air, sifted into the cabin. Outside, the shadows of the cat's claw bushes reached gnarled talons toward the cabin, retreating reluctantly before the rising moon. A nightjar twittered softly.

Drackett blinked, then rubbed his eyes. *Was that shadow that large a moment ago?* he wondered, a stab of fear quickening his pulse. Almost of itself, his left hand eased his Starr revolver a little higher in his holster.

From behind him a voice with the age and gentle power of a shifting sand dune spoke. "You will remove your fingers very carefully from the pistol."

Drackett and McGinty both had the good sense to freeze where they were. Drackett's hand slipped up across his stomach. Making no sudden movements, both turned slowly around to see Pitahaya standing in the deepest shadow of the room. *How did he get there?* both men thought in unison, but their attention was more intently focused on the muzzle of the rifle Pitahaya held.

"Why have you called me to this meeting? I know you to be a seller of the water-that-burns-with-fire, but my people have no money with which to buy. And what means the little-death-carrier you sent which is now in the fire stick pointed at your belly? I have done speaking."

McGinty explained to the chief his plan to help the Mojaves know which coaches would be carrying the payroll shipments. With that much money, he explained, Pitahaya's people could buy rifles, whiskey—anything they wanted.

"And when the pony soldiers come against us, what then?"

"It won't last that long. Two or three times at the most, and your people can go to your mountain camps with enough money for supplies to stay a year. By then this will be forgotten."

"And why do you make war on your own people?"

"Because others have what should belong to me and I want it," McGinty said cautiously.

"Bah! You are no man of honor, Mig-In-Tee. But we will fight this fight, and we will go to the mountains to live better than we do now. I want fifty of the golden-sided rifle-that-shoots-many-times and twice ten hands of bullets for each."

"Fifty rifles and a hundred rounds of ammunition each?" exploded McGinty. "I don't want to make war on the whole state, I just want you to knock over a couple of stages!"

At the angry tone in Fancy Dan's voice, Drackett's hand crept back down toward the butt of the revolver. His fingertips had barely touched the wood of the grip when he felt the prick of a steel knife point on his neck and a chill of fear down his spine.

"I know, Mig-In-Tee, that you wish us to be blamed for doing evil for you. You say the army will not come before we have gone. This may be true, but still we will be ready to fight them or we will not walk the war trail with you."

"All right, fifty rifles and the ammunition," McGinty agreed. "But," he warned, "it will take some time; I can only give you ten rifles now."

Pitahaya grunted a reply which McGinty took for assent, and he continued, "Also, you must only attack those whom we say. I know about the two prospectors you killed. That's where you got the Winchester you're holding."

Pitahaya shrugged as if the matter was of complete indifference to him. "It may be so, who can say? The desert claimed them for its own, that is all. They were not wise in its ways."

"If we're agreed, then tell your friend there to take the knife out of Mike's neck," commanded McGinty, proud of himself for having noticed the Indian behind Drackett. The pressure of the knife point was withdrawn and Drackett, who had been holding his breath, sighed with relief.

"Now about those first ten rifles . . ." McGinty, who had turned to look with amusement at Drackett's wide eyes gleaming with fear, was startled to discover that Pitahaya was gone as soundlessly as he had come.

———

Nearly everything had been settled by the time Ling Chow cleared away the dishes and poured coffee into the fine china cups. They were not made to fit the finger of a blacksmith. They were made for the delicate hand of a woman.

The observation gave Josh determination to speak out. There was something that had troubled him ever since Callie's mare bolted with her on its back. Josh knew more than a little about horses, and he was certain that the flashy gray was not made for the young woman who sat across from him now.

He cleared his throat. "That's a fine-looking mare you've got, Miss Callie—" His voice trailed off. After all, the choice of a mount was a very personal thing, like the choice of a friend.

"She was a gift. I brought her with me," Callie said

abruptly, without a smile. Did she guess where he was leading?

"A fine animal for a bridle path in a park, no doubt." Josh glanced at Mr. Morris who understood completely and encouraged him with a nod.

"Yes. I spent many afternoons on her, with a friend at my side. I can ride as well as a woman with sight. What happened last Tuesday was just a fluke, Mr. Roberts. It might have happened to anyone."

"It *would* have happened to anyone, on that horse," Josh plunged ahead.

"There is nothing wrong with the horse. She was frightened by the snake, and—"

"And she almost got you killed," Josh interrupted.

Callie's voice quavered slightly. "It could have happened to anyone," she repeated. Defensive and frightened by the experience, she made an effort to convince herself.

"Not with the right mount," he said firmly. "I know a little about horses. That mare is too high-strung for this part of the country." He was careful not to add that the horse was too high-strung for Callie Morris.

"I am used to her," Callie argued with lifted chin.

"She'll get you killed," he repeated, determined to see the discussion through by the hint of helplessness in her voice. She did argue, but certainly she understood that he was telling her the truth.

"But I love riding; it is the only real freedom—" She faltered.

"Look, I watched those Dawson boys break a whole string down there." Excitement edged his voice. "They've got one little bay mare—a pretty thing, she is. Black mane and tail, black stockings and good feet. And she's the kind of horse that just *wants* to please. Miss Callie, I trimmed her feet, and she was just the sweetest thing—practically turned around and said thanks! I said to myself, 'Now, this is a horse a man could ride from here to Mexico and never feel it!' And she's careful. Watches where she's going. Mont James rode her all over these hills, and her ears were perked and listening to every word he said. And I told him, 'There's a horse for Miss Callie.' "

She sat silently as he paused and waited. A slight smile curved her lips. "Then . . . you aren't saying I should never ride again?"

"No, Miss Callie. You've just got the wrong animal for the territory. But there is a right one for you . . ."

Now she inclined her head toward her father, who had chosen not to enter into the discussion with his strong-willed daughter. "Papa, could you arrange . . . I mean, if I am going to be riding again in the desert, perhaps Shadow is *not* suitable. If Mr. Roberts says there is a horse which will be better . . ."

Now Josh pretended to convince Mr. Morris, who was relieved down to the ground. "She's a three-year-old. Mont James says he'd be happy to put a bit more time on her and then give your daughter a hand until they're acquainted. No two horses are ever broke alike, but I never saw a horse so willing."

"Well, then," Morris eyed Callie. "It's rare to find a filly so well-tempered. I'd be a fool to pass her by."

A smile of genuine relief filled Callie's face. "May we go now and see her? I could use a little walk after Ling's dinner."

"Now? After dark?" Josh was surprised by her eagerness, and pleased he had pursued the offer.

"The dark does not hinder me, Mr. Roberts . . . *Joshua*. I can lead if you like." She laughed lightly, at ease with her handicap. "And please call me Callie."

And so Callie Morris took Joshua's arm and strolled slowly toward the corral where the new horses milled around. Josh liked the warmth of her small hand on his arm, and so he did not tell her that the sky was lit up with stars that illuminated the world from one horizon to the other. Instead he let her guide him.

"This is going to be a real town someday," she said quietly. Thank you, Joshua, for agreeing to be the constable. My father really needs your help with this. I wasn't just trying to 'sweet-talk' you into doing something you didn't want to do."

His smile forgave her and he quipped, "Just so long as I don't have to do it forever!"

"You see that knoll over there?" Callie pointed and, indeed, there was a knoll to her right. "I told Papa that as soon as the mine pays off we are going to have a church there. You can't have a town without a church."

He chuckled. "In this town we'd better have a jail built first. You can't have a town without the law."

"No. First the church, so that the jail will more likely be empty." In the distance the low nicker of a horse was heard. Callie stopped and turned to face Joshua. "Thank you for what you did in there." Her voice was full of gratitude. "Pick had taken me riding before, but we didn't want to worry my father, so we kept it a secret. Even the time we found you dying in the desert . . ." Her face flushed. "I didn't know who you were then, of course."

Josh's mouth fell open. "So it was *you*!"

"After what happened this week, my father told me I

would not be allowed to ride here again," Callie continued. "He said the incident occurred because I am blind, and—well, I almost believed it myself. Anyway, thank you for—" She did not finish.

Josh placed his hand over hers lying lightly on his arm. "I reckon you can do almost anything better than any other woman I know." Could she tell he was smiling at her? Did she know he wanted to kiss her?

She raised her face slightly as if to look at him, and he leaned toward her, smelling the fresh scent of lilacs. She smiled gently and lifted her chin toward him. He kissed her tenderly, and after a long moment she squeezed his arm.

"We'd best get back to the house now, Joshua," she said quietly. "But thank you—thank you for everything."

CHAPTER 9

"Big John," said Josh to Daniels, still chained to the post of his improvised jail, "aren't you about ready to get loose from there?"

"You got that right! I been here a month, seems like, an' I keep thinkin' 'bout them creepy-crawlers, so's at night I don't sleep much."

"You know, they told me they were gonna send for a judge or deputy for your case. But now I hear tell they've got some kind of inquest going into the death of two prospectors found over by Three Kill Spring. Nobody seems to know what to do about you, much less care, but I personally don't like the idea of leaving you tied up. Now if I cut you loose, are you gonna take out after my hide again?"

"Ah, *naw*, Josh! Shucks, you been right good to me. Feedin' me and fixin' this here tent an' all. I figger as off my head as I was, I coulda wound up shot and throwed to the coyotes. I only gets mean like that when I mix it up with the tangle-leg. Then I wants to mix it up with ever'body."

"Yeah, I figured that out. You ought to stay away from that rattlesnake juice."

"I try to, Josh; I really do. But when I'm a'workin' the forge, an' he comes by an' says, 'Come on, Big John, come and wet your whistle,' why I just natur'ly did what he said. An' he kep' sayin', 'Drink up, plenty more where that come from,'—shoot fire, I'se too far gone by then to see straight, much less stop."

"You keep referring to 'he,' Big John; who is 'he?' Who gave you the whiskey?"

"I thought you know'd, Josh. It was Beldad, the night foreman."

———

Before they'd reached a final agreement, Josh had given Morris two conditions for accepting the job of constable. The first was that Big John Daniels be reinstated as blacksmith. Morris agreed only after Josh assured him he would take full responsibility. The second was that Josh be given a week with Pickax to learn the ways of the desert.

As the two approached Pick's camp, the old man made a wide sweep with his arm in a gesture of welcome. "All right, boy, if you've a mind to study the desert, just remember that she don't take foolin' with. You gotta go with her, not agin her."

With no more preamble than this remark, the lessons had begun. Pick started by asking if Josh knew why the camp was located in this spot, and why the tent flap opened in the direction it did. The miner nodded his approval when Josh explained correctly that the campsite was shaded from the afternoon heat by the shadow of the overhanging bluff, and that the tent opening was such that it kept the prevailing wind from filling the tent with sand.

The two reached the tent and unsaddled their mounts. Josh gathered some dry mesquite branches, then collected some of the fleshy bulbs of prickly pears, as he had been instructed. "What do you want these for?" he asked curiously as the miner got a fire going.

"Lot's of good in a cactus, boy. Look here." Pickax proceeded to singe the barbs off the plant before tossing it to the ground. Jenny eagerly began to nibble the cactus shoots before they were completely cooled. Then Josh's horse Injun followed suit.

"Desert-bred critters can usually forage for themselves," commented Pick, "but sometimes we help 'em out a mite."

———

The next few days passed quickly with Pick proving an apt instructor and Josh an eager pupil. He learned which trees indicated the presence of moisture beneath the sand, and how to keep himself and his horse fed.

Pick told Josh to gather mesquite beans, which could be eaten, and pointed out the value of lizards for roasted meat. Josh also learned of a good poultice for snakebite—chewing tobacco.

"You gotta watch out for them little sidewinders and Mojave greens," warned Pick. "They hide in the sand with just their eyeballs out. And they don't give no warning before they take out after you, neither."

———

The one topic Pick laid the most stress on was the need for preparation and planning. "I seen people come to grief out here who shoulda knowed better. Like they was countin' on findin' water at a certain tank, and it was dry. They shoulda planned for that! They shoulda kept back enough water to get them by to the next spring."

"But what if that hole was dry too, Pick; what then? How can you plan for that?"

"Why shoot, boy, in that case they better be planned up on how they's gonna meet their Maker, 'cause they shore nuff will be seein' Him pronto. The trick, though, is doin' your plannin' so you don't see Him too soon!

"I seen men crazy fer water drinkin' sand, an' I seen men drink horse blood so's they could make one more sunset.

"Just remember, a man with a mount an' water is home safe. A man with only his horse or only his water can tough it through. But a man with neither horse nor water is a *dead man!*"

Whenever Pick saw that he was dishing out information faster than Josh could take it in, he'd call a halt to their classroom time. Then they'd retreat up the draw behind Pick's camp for a little shotgun practice. Josh had not carried the greener around town, but in his new job as constable, he agreed with Morris and Pickax that he should carry a weapon.

"No, boy, no, ya gotta clamp that scatter gun tight against your side, less'n you want to be missin' some teeth when she goes off!"

Josh quickly concluded that there weren't many fine points to blasting away with a sawed-off shot gun. The idea seemed to be to point the greener in the general direction of the target and keep a good hold on it so it wouldn't leap out of your hands when fired.

"This here rig is a whole sight better'n them old cap-fired models. Why, a man can load an' fire these little paper cartridges faster'n you can holler, *I quit!*"

Pick walked over to Josh's target area. "Looky here at this heap of prickly pear you just blasted. Throwed pieces out in all directions an' ain't any of them pieces too big, neither!" He laughed and shook his head.

"Remember son, a six-gun'll give you a scratch, but buckshot means buryin'."

CHAPTER 10

Josh took to his new duties with sincere interest, if not enthusiasm. He practiced the frontier proverb, *You play the hand you're dealt;* only he would have said, *You shoe the horse they bring you.*

The merchants and townspeople were, for the most part, supportive of his appointment. They saw the establishment of a full-time peacekeeping position as one more step toward civilization, respectability—even permanence. Jacobson, the hardware store owner, was especially agreeable.

"Yah, dis a great day for Garson. We haf ben mit out a lawman long enuff, und de riff-raff is gettin' too big mit der britches, yah?"

"*For* their britches, Mr. Jacobson," Josh corrected. "But I hope you don't expect the town to change overnight just because I'm around. As long as there's drinking and miners mixed together, there's always a match to the dynamite, I think."

"Yah, but you are de strong breath to blow out dis metch. You, und dat cannon you have der—" He gestured toward the shotgun that Josh carried muzzle downward by a sling around his right shoulder.

Josh reached over with his left hand and grasped the greener around its stock. "You're right about that. Even folks who'd argue with me don't care to get into a dispute with this."

Their conversation was interrupted by the sound of gunfire. A man Josh recognized as an employee at the Red Dog Saloon burst out of the swinging doors and ran up to him. "Hey, aint'cha the new constable?"

"That's me. What's the trouble?"

"You better come with me, pronto. There's this Texican shootin' up the place!"

Josh moved cautiously toward the saloon while Mr. Jacobson dashed inside his store and bolted the door.

"Whoopee! Ah'm the original, double tough, quick as a rattler, death-dealer! Whoopee!" With the second yell came another gunshot that shattered the Red Dog's front window and made curious citizens across the street run for cover.

Josh had unslung the shotgun and held it at ready as he crouched beside the building, but his mind was racing, looking for some way to avoid a shootout.

"Barkeep! Barkeep, I say! I don't like the looks of that lady's pit'cher up thar. She's lookin' at me funny. Turn her face to the wall, Barkeep, and be quick about it."

Josh peered cautiously around the corner through the broken window, and saw the drunken man holding a six-gun on the trembling bartender as the latter tried to reach a painting hanging over the bar. When he still could not reach it after climbing up on the shelves of liquor, the Texan said, "Let's see y'all jump for it," and he fired another round, just barely missing the bartender's foot. The bartender fell sideways in a crash of bottles, smashing three shelves down to the floor.

Josh knew it was only a matter of time before somebody started shooting in earnest. Hanging the shotgun back over his shoulder, he stood up and called loudly into the saloon.

"Where you at, you old cuss? Hey, don't be bustin' up all them bottles, save some for me!"

The Texan whirled around and stood swaying slightly as if pondering this interruption.

Josh gave him no time to respond. "Where you been keepin' yourself? Why, I ain't seen you since Waco. How ya been?"

The cowboy's eyes squeezed shut, then opened slowly and focused on Josh with difficulty. A gambler was hiding under a table by Josh's feet as he stepped over the window sill and into the saloon. He called out, "Shoot him, shoot him quick!" He was silenced by Josh's sudden kick into his midsection.

Josh continued to address the drunk in a loud voice. "Still usin' that same ol' Colt, ain't you? Danged if it ain't a fine piece. Is your eye as good as it was when y'all shot twelve bullseyes runnin' at that turkey shoot on the Brazos?"

The Texan considered this question by looking down at the Colt in his hand, then back at Josh. He nodded slowly, then yelled, "Wanta see? Prop up one of 'em tinhorn gamblers. I'll shoot out his gold fillin's!"

"Naw, old hoss, now that ain't no contest. See if you can shoot the flies offa the top of that wall there." Josh waved toward the side wall of the saloon, away from the street and the rest of the town.

The Texan squinted his eyes and then remarked with confidence, "Ah'll take the one on the left first!" and he fired another shot that hit high on the wall.

"Dogged if'n you didn't nail him. Can you catch his friend there, too?"

Without further comment, the cowboy fired again and with evident satisfaction, yelled, "Whoopee! I kin lick my weight in wildcats, an' shoot faster'n greased lightning, I—"

Josh added quickly, "Hey, hoss, that little one up there's gettin' away."

"No, he ain't!" shouted the Texan, and "click" went the hammer on an empty chamber.

"Grab him, boys," ordered Josh, and the cowering drinkers and gamblers wasted no time in subduing the cowboy.

"Don't hurt him," cautioned Josh. "Tie him up and bring me his rig. Take him upstairs and let him sleep it off, then let's see about cleaning up this mess."

———

"What about that Roberts fellow?" McGinty asked Beldad.

Mike Drackett leaned forward in his chair and grinned. "Lemme take care of him, Boss. I been itchin' for the chance."

McGinty spun his office chair around to face Drackett. "No, you ignorant lunk, do you want to really unite this town against us? I don't mean *eliminate* him, I'm talking about *recruiting* him!"

Drackett snorted, "Him? He's Morris's right-hand man after savin' that blind gal. What's more, I hear tell he's sweet on her. I can take him, Boss, I know I can. Lemme just solve this problem once and for all!"

McGinty wasn't so quick to reply this time. "Not now, not yet," he muttered. "Not while he's riding so high and has those friends in town. The Dawsons are no folks we want to cross. We'll give Beldad a chance to sound Roberts out, and wait for those cowboys to get out of town. All right, Beldad?"

"Sure, Mr. McGinty, anything you say. But Mike here is right. Roberts can't be bought, I'm thinkin'."

"Everyone has his price," murmured Fancy Dan softly. "We just have to find out what his might be."

————

At twilight Josh was leaning against the wall outside Jacobson's Hardware, watching the progress of traffic up and down the road. Despite rumblings from the working men of Garson about the upcoming layoff, no violence had broken out, and the town seemed calm.

Beldad approached Josh from across the street. "Hello, Roberts," he said.

"Beautiful evening, Mr. Beldad. Are you headed up to work?"

"Directly, directly. Time enough for a drink first. Thought I'd ask you to join me."

"No, thank you, Mr. Beldad. I believe I'll just stay here and enjoy the evening."

Despite this refusal, Beldad gave no indication of intending to move on. Instead he moved closer to Josh and dropped his voice.

"You know, there's something I've been meaning to speak to you about, having to do with the welfare of this town and the mine and all."

"Yes, Mr. Beldad. What might that be?"

"The men are not going to stand for this unfair treatment by Morris. You can see they'll be able to prevent any work from being done at all if Morris doesn't change his mind. Anyway, it's important for us to know where you stand."

"I'm curious about who *us* might be, Mr. Beldad, but then you haven't been exactly keeping your sentiments quiet. Even though you're a foreman, you belong to the so-called Working Men of Garson, don't you?"

"There is no shame in being connected with a group who are standing up for their rights and demanding fair treatment."

"No, that's correct as you have described it. But what I see of these who style themselves Working Men is a group of loud-mouthed bullies. Your group, Mr. Beldad, seems to contain a high percentage of men who were already discharged for drunkenness or loafing or being general troublemakers. I'll bet the actual number of single miners who wholeheartedly support you is very small indeed."

"And you, Roberts? Aren't you single? Or are you special since you been sparking that blind girl? It don't hurt your standing with—"

Beldad's words were cut off mid-sentence as Josh lifted the man by his shirtfront so that only his boot tips touched the planks.

"Beldad, I'm going to tell you this just once: your opinions about me are of no interest to me. But let me hear tell of you bad-mouthing Miss Callie—just once, and not only will I thrash you within an inch of your life, but I'll tie a can to your tail and stone you out of town like the miserable cur you are! Now get out of my sight!" Josh let Beldad drop so abruptly that instead of landing upright, Beldad missed his footing and landed heavily, seat first, on the boardwalk.

"You better watch yourself, Roberts," snarled Beldad. "You'll be sorry you didn't listen to me. You'll see you can't treat me like this!"

Roberts turned slowly to stare down at Beldad, who for all his tough talk had not risen to his feet to speak his piece. "Should I consider that a threat, Mr. Beldad?"

"A warning, call it. You'll be sorry!"

"Beldad, I'm already sorry I didn't run you out of town before now! Get out of here before I change my mind and start looking for the can and string!"

Beldad scrambled to his feet and made a quick exit in the opposite direction, cursing and muttering all the way.

CHAPTER 11

Josh patrolled Garson's street for a few uneventful days. Then he looked up one morning to see Mont James sauntering toward him with a cat-that-got-the-canary grin on his face.

Before Mont could speak, Josh held up his hand. "Don't tell me; let me guess. You've unloaded all those spavined, jug-headed death-on-four-feet critters on some poor, unsuspecting greenhorns."

Mont's grin grew still wider, his eyes dancing with merriment. "All right; you're so all-fired smart, you tell me the rest."

Josh mused a minute, then continued, "And instead of making a down payment at Freeman's Mortuary, like they ought to before forkin' one of your widow-makers, they paid in cash!"

Mont's smile fairly reached from ear to ear, but he only replied, "Now you're with it, brother; preach on, preach on!"

"And, and . . . what else is there?"

Mont raised his eyebrows expectantly.

"You don't mean—you got more buyers than you had horses!"

"You can put a big 'Amen!' to that, brother Joshua!" Mont dropped his exaggerated accent. "We sold every head out of this string and we're heading back out for more!"

"That's great news, Mont. Will you and Tom and Nate be leaving right away?"

"Yes, but we're going home first. Tom's been missing Miss Emily something fierce. We've been on the dry side of those peaks for better'n a month now, and some things up yonder need tending to. We figure to be back in two or three weeks and get another roundup and breaking done before the snow flies."

Josh stuck out his hand. "I hate to see you go, Mont. You and your family have been about the only ones in this town who aren't either crazy or scared or angry about something."

Mont grasped Josh's hand and looked directly into his friend's eyes and replied, "Josh, you and me, we work around horses and we know how tricky they can be and how ornery and how powerful. But sooner or later, they all come around to being broke to ride. How is that, do you figure?"

Josh wasn't sure where this twist in the conversation was leading, but he found himself nodding thoughtfully and answering, "I guess some horses figure out sooner than others that you're going to feed them as well as break them, and that for a little cooperation they can get a lot of care."

Mont nodded. "And do we try to take all the spirit out of 'em?"

"Naw, no way. You just try to break their will to fight back, not destroy their spirit. Why, a horse with no spirit is as worthless as a nag that's never been broke, only in a different way."

"Exactly." Mont smiled.

"What do you mean, *exactly*? I don't know what you're getting at."

"You said everybody in Garson is angry or fretted or crazy. The truth is, they've never been broke; they're still fighting the bit and kicking the saddle to flinders."

"Broke? Broke by who?"

"Come on now, Josh. You told me your mama raised you in the church. You know what I'm driving at. The Lord Jesus is just waiting for a chance to care for them and teach them and take the fret out of their lives, but first they've gotta get their muliness broke down to size, so He can build up their good qualities from there."

"Yeah, I see what you mean. Just like breaking horses, huh?"

"Yep. Except for one little thing."

"What might that be?"

"When I go to break a horse, I don't ask his permission. But when God wants to make someone over, He can't even begin till they ask Him."

"Are you saying I need to ask Him?"

"Well, Josh, only you and the Lord Jesus know about that. But I know you're headed His way. God's got big plans for you, Josh Roberts, and He isn't through putting the school on you, yet!"

Mont pumped Josh's hand again and added, "You be extra careful, Mr. Constable. I want to see this town prosper and get civilized so they'll buy more horses. I figure the town needs you to guide it along." He slapped Josh on the shoulder. "If you need us sooner than a month, just give a holler and we'll come running. Be seeing you, Josh."

———

The stage from Mojave was running late. The connecting stage from San Bernadino was delayed, and the driver from Mojave had no choice but to wait. The connecting stage carried the payroll, some two thousand dollars in gold coin, for the Silver Rim in Garson.

The driver was a five-year veteran of this desert run. A short, stocky man with a loud voice and a swaggering walk, his name was Hurry Johnson. He enjoyed the task of guiding the four-up team of mules through the arid country. Much of the terrain was flat, allowing many opportunities for speed, and speed was what Hurry Johnson lived for.

Hurry was a great admirer of the exploits of Hank Monk and other line handlers whose daring—if not insane—driving had made them legendary. For all that he imitated of their style, Hurry didn't care about achieving fame; the chance to drive fast as often as possible was reward enough.

In spite of his emphasis on speed, Hurry was a skilled professional, constantly asking questions of the other drivers to improve his knowledge of the conditions of the road. But he was not given to worrying about what he considered idle speculation, so when he heard talk of Indian activity, he was skeptical.

"Them Mojaves ain't got grit enough to attack a stage with a armed driver and guard. Their style is more pickin' on lonely old dirt-poor prospectors an' toothless dogs," he said.

He was told that some stretches of the trail toward the silver mining country were watched by Mojaves. It was not uncommon to see small clusters of Indians making their way from place to place, but they had never seemed to be concerned about the passage of the red and yellow coaches that spattered them with gravel and left them in the dust.

"Lately they been watchin' us, but it ain't like them to be movin' much in the heat of day," he was told.

Hurry discounted all this talk. He knew stage drivers craved adventure. The plain fact was, most of the present bunch had grown up too late for much of the excitement in the West. Now the really long trips were all made by train, and even little out-of-the-way one-horse towns were getting civilized. Hurry figured that any talk of Indian trouble was a result of wishful but fanciful thinking. Anyway, speed was where real adventure could be found. "Aah," he snorted, "I can outrun a Mojave any day."

His guard for this trip was a young man, Oliver de la Fontaine by name. Folks around said Oliver was too short by half for such a long name, but if they did make that observation they did so out of his hearing. Oliver was a slight young man of nineteen, but he had "killed his man" when he was only seventeen and was known to be a practiced hand with the Smith and Wesson he brought west with him from Boston.

For this trip he was carrying a shotgun, as stagecoach guards often did, but he still wore the S and W at his side. Hurry was impatient to be off, so when the inbound coach finally did arrive, he barely grunted in greeting before throwing the mail pouches and the payroll bag into the boot. He snapped its cover down and had it half secured when he was told that he also would have a passenger with some luggage.

Hurry ripped back the canvas with a violent yank that indicated how irritated he was. When the trunk had been deposited, he wasted no time in tightening the leather straps and buckles, then vaulted into his seat.

A kick to the brake lever and a slap of the reins and they were off, with Oliver making a quick grab at his hat and their solitary passenger being seated somewhat more abruptly than he had intended.

This was a good stretch of road to make up time, and Hurry proceeded to take advantage of it. The road skirted the mesquite and yucca-covered foothills east of the Sierra Nevadas as it ran northward. The land was not flat, but the rises and washes were gentle enough to cause little loss of speed. Behind the coach rose a dust cloud twenty feet high that trailed them for a quarter of a mile as they sped along.

To reach the first stop at Weidner's was only a matter of an hour or so. The team was not changed here; they were just given a little water and a chance to breathe before the run was resumed.

The next hour contained both faster and slower passages. The road crossed deeper washes that flooded when the thunder crashed over the Sierra peaks. These canyons not only had steeper sides, but sandy bottoms that slowed the team as resistance to the coach's wheels increased.

Slowing down was something Hurry did reluctantly, but he knew a driver who had dumped a coach in an attempt to use too much speed in one of these arroyos. Hurry hadn't particularly thought the wreck was a tragedy; what bothered him was that the driver had been fired and had been forced to leave this area to get work. So in the plunges into the canyons, Hurry used more caution than he really wanted.

These periods of slower travel were compensated by the times when the stage road ran through the alkali flats. Formed when the occasional flood burst out of the confining arroyos, the flats could be as much as a mile wide. The mineral-laden water which pooled in these areas was either absorbed into the soil or evaporated, leaving behind a crust of alkali salts which formed a hard, shiny surface on which almost nothing grew.

On these stretches Hurry was really in his element. He urged the team to greater and greater speed, and they responded till the coach fairly flew over the ground. A grin would break out on Hurry's features as if the force of the wind itself had pulled the corners of his mouth back toward his ears.

Oliver had ridden with Hurry enough to be nonchalant about this breakneck charge across the desert. Passengers, on the other hand, were so often unprepared for the intensity of the rush that they remained unable to speak or relax their white-knuckled grips on their valises for several minutes after reaching Red Rock Station.

There the team was changed, and sometimes mail and passengers exchanged. The road also split at this point, turning aside toward Garson from the main track that continued on north to Indian Wells.

From the station eastward through Red Rock Canyon, Hurry's face resumed its normal, uninspired look. The twists and turns of the road as it followed the wash through sandstone ledges never allowed for the velocity Hurry craved. Passengers might enjoy the orange and pink formations and comment on the colorful bands stretched on either side of the road, but Hurry took no pleasure in sightseeing.

As the coach turned into the third in a series of S-shaped curves leading through the canyon, Oliver leaned over and observed, "You know, Hurry, I think I saw an

Injun up top of that rock. Isn't this the stretch where Murchison said he saw those Mojaves?"

"I reckon. I never paid him no mind, anyways. What d'ya figger the Injun was doin'?"

"I don't know, but let me get Betsy here limbered up anyway," said Oliver as he took the shotgun out of its rest beside his seat and checked its loads.

"Hey, in there!" Oliver called to the passenger. "Look sharp! There may be some trouble up ahead. If you got a piece, get it ready." The message produced more than just startled consternation, for in a moment a hand protruded from the driver's side window holding a .45 caliber Colt.

The stage entered the next turn, slowing to a cautious pace, then speeding up as the corner was made and the way shown to be clear. "Twern't nothin' to it, after all," grunted Hurry. "Mebbe you had a speck o' dust in your eye."

Oliver was about to agree when a rifle shot struck the seat between the two men, splintering the underside of the board. Oliver whirled around to catch a glimpse of a Mojave on an overhead sandstone ledge just as he directed another shot at them. He returned one barrel of the shotgun at the attacker, more in hope of spoiling the Indian's aim than of hitting him, then immediately emptied the second barrel at another Mojave on the opposite canyon wall. This time the blast made its mark as the Indian clutched his chest and tumbled forward off the rocks.

Hurry snapped the reins and cursed the mules into a sudden burst of speed. They needed no urging as they caught the nervous excitement of rifle fire popping around them.

The passenger was firing now also, taking deliberate aim as well as he could from the pitching and careening coach. The sandstone walls seemed to have sprouted Mojaves; half a dozen were firing from either side of the arroyo. The passenger's last shot took out an Indian who was firing down on the coach, but not before a .44 slug tore behind Hurry's left shoulder and dug a furrow down his back.

From the sudden curse that burst from his lips and clenched teeth, Oliver knew Hurry had been hit. "Shall I take the lines?" he shouted.

"I can drive with my teeth if I have to. Just you keep 'em offa me, an' I'll get us outta here." Other shots hit the coach as he spoke.

The fact was, the coach had already swept past all but the last pair of Mojaves. Although the occupants of the stage couldn't have known it at the time, the Indians had been unsure of their strategy and had relied too much on new weapons with which they were not yet very familiar.

Oliver fired his S and W at the last Indian on his side when both Mojaves leaped from their rocky perches toward the speeding stage coach. One landed on top of the coach, but was slung over the side as they jolted around a curve. The Indian caught himself just before being thrown off and began to pull himself back up over the side. Oliver leveled his pistol at the Indian's head, but the hammer snapped on an empty chamber as he pulled the trigger. He instinctively reached for the shotgun which lay at his feet. Swinging it by the barrel, his gun stock's blow swept the Mojave backwards and off the coach, bouncing him against the rocky wall and onto his face in the sand.

The other Indian, landing further back on the stage's roof, did not attempt to attack either driver or guard. He had made his leap with a knife clenched in his fist, and he used it now to slit open the canvas covering of the boot.

After knocking the one Mojave clear of the coach, Oliver had crammed two more shells into the shotgun and clambered to the roof. He was surprised to see the Indian crouching in the boot, throwing out the passenger's trunk and mailbag, then raising the payroll pouch to throw it off. At Oliver's involuntary shout, the Indian looked up, poised to throw his knife. Oliver's shotgun, no more than four feet away, blew him right off the back.

Hurry never let up on the mules until they had exited the canyon and put some miles of open space between themselves and the attack. Then he pulled up to rest the lathered and trembling team and allowed Oliver to examine and bandage his wound. The bullet had torn the flesh clear down to Hurry's hip where it had glanced off a bone before exiting.

"Looks to me like this'll be more trouble to your sitting back in a chair than it will to your driving," observed Oliver.

"I coulda told you that," said Hurry, through gritted teeth. "Ain't nothin' keeps me from drivin'."

"I can't imagine where the Mojaves got those rifles, but it was lucky for us they weren't too good at using them!"

"More'n that, it's lucky they didn't hit the mules. Likely they was tryin' not to hit 'em, so's they could drive 'em back to their camp and make a meal of 'em."

"Did you ever know these Indians to attack a stage before?"

"Never. Mostly they stay clear of folks that can fight back, but this bunch had a plan to take us out."

"Suppose they knew about the payroll shipment?"

"How in tarnation could an Injun know about that? That last 'un was likely trying to get whatever he could, since they couldn't stop us."

"You know, we were downright lucky. Helped to have that passenger shooting on your side of the coach."

"Ain't that the truth! Say, why haven't we heard from him?"

Oliver and Hurry looked at each other as the same thought struck them. Neither were surprised when Oliver opened the stagecoach door to find the passenger's lifeless body sprawled across the seats. Two of the Indians' .44 slugs had made their marks after all.

CHAPTER 12

Callie was sitting in her carriage, waiting for Ling Chow's return, when Fancy Dan walked up beside her.

"Miss Morris, a word with you, if you please?"

"Yes, Mr. McGinty, what is it?"

"It never ceases to amaze me how you can tell in an instant who a person is by their voice alone."

"Is that what you wanted to tell me, Mr. McGinty?"

"Why, no, no it's not. I actually wanted to say—well, what I intended to ask was . . ."

"Come now, Mr. McGinty, bashfulness is hardly your style," remarked Callie dryly. "What is on your mind?"

"You certainly are a direct person, Miss Morris; I like that. All right, I'll be direct as well. I'd like to call on you at your home, to get to know you better. You are a lovely and well-spoken woman, and I'd like to—"

"Thank you, Mr. McGinty, I believe I understand your question. To be equally straightforward, your interest does not interest me. No thank you."

"Ah, but, Miss Morris—may I call you Callie?"

"I'd rather you didn't, Mr. McGinty."

McGinty continued smoothly, as if he hadn't detected the snub, "Miss Morris, I believe that I can offer you refined, intelligent conversation. What's more, I am a man of ambition. I expect to own a fine home in San

146

Francisco; perhaps enter politics."

"And then what, Mr. McGinty?"

McGinty's smoothness wavered. "What?" he demanded. Then catching himself, he said soothingly, "Pardon me, I didn't quite catch what you asked?"

"Then what?" she repeated. "What are you doing that will outlast your saloon in Garson, your fine home in San Francisco, and even your ambition?"

In what was a most unusual circumstance for him, McGinty was momentarily speechless. He decided to ignore this baffling discussion and try a different approach.

"Your friend Roberts may style himself a constable, but he's really just a sweaty blacksmith. He won't ever be able to treat you to the kind of genteel life you deserve."

This may have been straight talk, but it was entirely the wrong tactic to take with Callie Morris. She stiffened noticeably, and whether intentionally or not, she managed to turn so that the brilliant sunlight reflected off her smoked glasses directly into McGinty's eyes. He blinked and fidgeted uncomfortably, but she tilted her head to follow the sound, so that the irritation continued. "That is not even remotely any of your business, Mr. McGinty. Now, good day to you."

"Miss Morris, you shouldn't be so hasty. After all, my attention might benefit your father. You do care about your father, don't you? Indeed, one might say that a disregard for my attentions could be, shall we say, *unpleasant* for your father."

Callie's remaining patience snapped at this poorly veiled threat. She stood in the carriage, her hand finding the buggy whip that rested at her side. She snatched the whip up and snapped it into the air. McGinty leaped back out of its way, but not before the stinging lash caught his ear. "Mr. McGinty," she said slowly and deliberately, "do not threaten me or my father. And if you know what's good for you, never speak to me again."

At that moment Ling Chow hurried out of the hardware store. "What going on here? Miss Callie, what you do?" He climbed in beside her and took the reins.

"Ah, Ling Chow, Mr. McGinty asked my opinion of something, and I was *giving it to him*." Callie flung the whip down on the leather seat.

McGinty, now that he was safely out of range, had recovered his aplomb. Holding a silk handkerchief to his bleeding earlobe, he sneered, "You shouldn't be so high and mighty, Miss Morris; and you *won't* be soon. If you're lucky, I might give you a job in my casino making change for gamblers. I guess even a blind girl could do that."

Callie turned her face from him. "Drive us home, Ling," she said through stiff lips. She could hear McGinty's mocking laughter behind her as the team stepped out smartly and drew the carriage up the street.

"But what did he mean, Papa? How can he hurt us?"

"Hush now, child, he can't hurt us. He's just a no-good, rotten bully and a cheap crook with a two-bit way of talking."

"Papa, you're not telling me everything. How can he even think to turn us out?"

Morris sighed heavily, and taking Callie's hands in his, led her over to the settee. "All right, Callie, you deserve an explanation. Sit down here."

"First of all, McGinty has nothing on us, and you

mustn't fret about it. But he has made an offer to the Golden Bear Company to purchase the Silver Rim."

"Buy the Rim? But Papa, you're a Director of the Golden Bear."

"Yes, Callie, that's true. But I'm only one of many. You know the Rim's been losing money, and—well, McGinty's offer was substantial enough that the other directors have voted to consider it."

"Just like that? Without even thinking of us and all the work you've done?"

"Now simmer down, California. No, it's not just like that. The directors have agreed to give me a little more time to prove my belief in the quality of the ore the Rim can produce. Unfortunately, they're not willing to give me very long, and you know the setbacks we've been having."

"Yes, and I bet McGinty's behind them, too!"

"I'm sure he's encouraged the talk of unrest among the men I laid off. But, Callie, he can't have been responsible for the loss of the payroll in the Indian attack. No, even McGinty wouldn't stoop that low."

"All right, Papa. You know, you shouldn't keep things from me. Anyway, I can always tell when you're upset. But how can I pray for you if I don't know what to pray about?"

"Lord love you, child, you're right. Let's both do some praying right now. If God is willing, we won't have any more trouble, and the Rim will make this town bloom— but it won't be by the likes of Fancy Dan McGinty running things!"

CHAPTER 13

Heading back to town on foot after another evening with Callie, Josh tried to analyze how he felt. Warmth flooded him, like the instant sense of heat when gray clouds part and sunshine bathes your face. The sensation felt unfamiliar, like waking up in a new place and not knowing for a time where you are. And it felt scary, like having the responsibility to care for something precious beyond measure. He was in love!

"Injun," he spoke to his horse, which he was leading behind him, "do you suppose everyone who's in love feels like this all the time? How do they ever get any work done?"

The horse nickered softly as if to reply, *Who knows? Wait and see, and enjoy the waiting.*

Josh shut his eyes and stood still, absorbing the night sounds, senses, and smells. He continued on down the road toward town, still walking and leading Injun. Riding would cut short the time he wanted to spend thinking.

He had just passed the turn in the trail which hid the Morris home from Garson when the buckskin whinnied again softly, then louder.

Off to his right, another horse answered! Josh couldn't have said why, but instinctively he knew something was wrong, and in that knowing he reacted.

Josh swung Injun around on the lead rope, the horse prancing nervously. He slipped the straps of the greener and the cartridge pouch off the saddle horn, and as he thumbed back one hammer, something whistled just past his ear, and a muzzle flash and report of a pistol came from the darkness.

Josh swung up the greener and fired from the hip as Pick had taught him, directly back toward the unseen attacker. Then he flung himself to the ground as Injun pounded off, back up toward the Morris home.

A second shot and a third went over Josh's head as he lay on the ground. From the two flashes Josh could see that his attacker was circling to the left, apparently moving to get a clean shot at Josh's side.

Josh pulled back the other hammer, pointed the shotgun's muzzle along the road, and lay very still. An instant later his guess was proven correct as a boot crunched the gravel of the road not ten yards away.

Josh didn't wait for his assailant to fire, but blasted off the second barrel, immediately rolling to the other side of the road as he did. His fire was met with an agonized scream and a wild return shot that ricocheted off a rock beside the road and went singing off into the dark. An instant searing pain, like a hot iron, leaped across Josh's forehead. A second later, Josh heard the sounds of feet running clumsily and a continuous string of curses.

Joshua fumbled in the cartridge bag. His nervous fingers spilled three shells on the road, then closed on two more as he broke open the shotgun's action and replaced the spent ammunition with fresh.

Lying still in the slight depression beside the road, Josh could hear the retreating footfalls stop, and then more cursing and shuffling as his attacker tried to get a spooked horse to stand still. The sound of saddle leather creaking suggested that the man, whoever he was, had succeeded. This was confirmed a moment later; hoof-beats retreated rapidly toward town.

Joshua stood up slowly and felt himself grow dizzy. He put his hand up to his forehead, and it came away wet and sticky to his touch.

From up the road came Morris's voice, "Joshua, are you there? Joshua, answer me! Ling Chow, have that rifle ready!"

"Ready, Mistah Mollis! Let Ling go fust!"

Josh called out to them, "It's all right. I'm here. Someone shot at me, but he's run off now."

Morris and the Chinaman hurried up, and as Morris stooped to light the lantern he carried, Josh could see a six-gun in his hand. The Chinaman was armed with a Henry rifle.

Morris stood up. "Are you hurt, my . . . good *grief*, your face is all bloody! Sit down, or, or . . . lie down! Ling, fetch the wagon. No, we'll carry you."

"It's all right, Mr. Morris, it's only a scratch; I'm just a little dizzy. There, that'll do for now," said Josh, as he clamped a neckerchief over the wound.

Morris and Ling Chow walked on either side of Josh as they returned to the house. Callie was standing in the doorway, her face a mask of worry and concern. She called out as she heard the returning footsteps, "Is he all right, Papa?"

Mr. Morris and Joshua exchanged looks that said, *She really cares* and *Let's not worry her.* Morris replied, "Yes, Callie, Joshua chased the other man off, and he's coming back with us."

Once inside the house, Josh was forced to admit to his forehead wound, and Callie immediately took charge. Leading him to the kitchen where she could get warm water, she sat him down on a short stool. Bathing his forehead, she instructed Josh to hold a clean compress on it while she washed the rest of his face. With strong, steady fingers, she gently traced the edges of the wound and announced with relief that it was, indeed, only a grazing.

Josh nodded thoughtfully. "I don't even think it's a bullet wound. A chunk of rock must have flown up from his last shot."

"Maybe—but, oh Josh, *who* would want to *kill* you? It *could* have been a bullet!"

Josh reached up and took her slender hand in his. "God watches out for me, Callie; you told me that yourself this very evening. As to who did it, that's exactly what I aim to find out!"

The next day Josh made his way around Garson with his forehead bandaged, asking questions. He wanted to know who had been seen coming back to town with a fresh wound.

Among the merchants, no one knew anything or had seen anything unusual, and there was no reason to think they would cover up for anyone. Doctor Racine examined the patch job Callie had done on Josh's forehead, but vowed he'd had no late-night patients with gunshot wounds. "I'll sure let you know if anyone shows up. Any idea what sort of wound I should be looking for?"

Josh instinctively rubbed his forehead, which had a dull ache. "Whoever it was made it back to his horse all right and rode off, but his last shot was wild and he didn't fire again. I'd say it's good odds he's at least hit on his gun hand side."

"Good enough; I'll be looking out for him."

Josh was hesitant to tackle the saloons. There he expected a less cheerful reception. If the attack was connected with the growing dispute among the miners, members of the so-called Working Men were less likely to be helpful.

Might as well start off with the place I know will be the least troublesome, he told himself. Turning his steps up the brush-covered slope, he entered the No Name Saloon.

"Welcome, my friend, welcome!" burst out Jersey Smith, his pointed beard bobbing as he spoke. "What have we here? I perceive some jealous female has attempted to scratch out your eyes!"

"Something like that, Jersey," remarked Josh, laying the greener on the bar top. "Can we visit quietly here for a minute?"

"Of course, my boy," agreed Jersey, lowering his voice. "Tell me what you need."

Josh recounted the story of the night before and ended by putting the question to Jersey about any man with a newly wounded right side or arm. Jersey thought carefully before answering, then shook his mane of white hair. "No— I've seen some wounds, but nothing of the sort you describe. Perhaps the ruffian has left town by now."

"I don't think so. I'm pretty certain he was acting on someone else's orders. They may try to get him out of town, but I was watching the road last night, and Dub Taylor's keeping an eye out today."

"He must be in hiding somewhere."

"That's what I think, too. I'm hoping that where I find him will tell me who's behind this."

"I'll be happy to be of service any way I can, but I really doubt that he'd show up here. As you know, I'm opposed to the group of hoodlums calling themselves Working Men, so they don't frequent my establishment."

"I figured as much, but I don't want to jump to conclusions and overlook something."

Josh turned around slowly and surveyed the small saloon. The men were all quietly talking or playing cards. Most of them were married, and those who were single were not known as troublemakers. Josh turned back to Jersey with a wry smile. "What I really mean is that I put off going into the lion's den long enough. Thanks for your help." Taking the shotgun from the bar top, he left through the tent flap.

Josh squared his shoulders and took a deep breath. It was time to get down to serious business. He went first into the Chinaman's Chance. Immediately he felt some hostility in the sidelong glances and whispered comments that passed among the miners. Even though Josh had been well-liked by all the miners, his position as constable with the full backing of the Silver Rim owner put him on the opposite side of the fence from the Working Men. Besides that, the fact that he was still employed while being a single man made for even more resentment.

No one knew anything about a wounded man, or if they did, they weren't saying. Josh located a few friendly faces to have a moment's conversation, but these men were subjected to intimidating stares for even giving the time of day to the constable. In any case, they added, they were moving on in a day or so to look for work in the mines around Independence.

That's just great, Josh mused, soberly shaking his head as he headed across the street toward Fancy Dan's. *Pretty soon the only single men left in Garson will be the ones who would rather drink and fight than do an honest day's work. I sure hope Mr. Morris is right about that big vein opening up soon. This town needs some good luck before it boils over.*

Josh thought he saw Beldad looking out the door at the front of Fancy Dan's, but the face disappeared too quickly for him to be sure. One thing was certain— McGinty had been warned about Josh's approach. He stepped up to shake Josh's hand before he was completely through the door.

"Well, Constable Roberts, what brings you in this time of day? Say, I'll bet you're looking for information about that drunken sot who took a shot at you last night. How is your head, anyway?"

"My head's fine, Mr. McGinty. I'm looking to find whoever that was last night all right, but how do you know he was drunk?"

McGinty scratched absently at his smooth-shaven cheek. "Heh! Well—I don't know for a fact, of course, just guessing. But it must have been someone who'd had more than was good for him. Perhaps it was some cowboy nursing a grievance against you."

"Mr. McGinty, what happened last night was an attempt at cold-blooded murder. I've Divine Providence to thank that I'm alive today. Drunk or not, an ambush is not the ploy of an angry cowboy. This was more like the move of someone following orders."

"Perhaps you're right," agreed McGinty hastily. "In

any case, how can I be of help?"

Josh was aware of the same hostile glances he had been subject to in the other saloon. There was an undercurrent of animosity which seemed to be directed at him personally—almost as if someone had been talking about him when he walked in.

When Josh spoke again it was in a calm, quiet voice. "I'll just have a look around, if you don't mind."

"Not at all, not at all. Help yourself."

Josh made a slow circuit of the room, getting angry looks and muttered half-hearted curses, but seeing no one with the kind of recent injury he sought. He returned to McGinty, who was standing at the bar, sharing a private word with the bartender and smiling at something.

Josh stopped and took a good look at the slick saloon-keeper, then remarked casually, "Guess I'll take a quick look upstairs."

McGinty reacted immediately. "Now, why would you want to do that? You can see I have nothing to hide. Besides, the activities upstairs are no concern of yours, if you know what I mean." He gave Josh a broad wink and a leering smile.

"I believe I'll have a look, just the same." Josh started for the stairs, and at the same moment the bartender, who had been arranging the bottles on a shelf behind the bar, knocked one over. It fell with a crash, amplified by its collision with a brass spittoon.

Josh whirled around, but the bartender merely lifted his palms and shrugged. Josh had his foot on the bottom step when a door at the head of the stairs opened, and one of the girls of the line came out, followed by Mike Drackett.

Drackett's voice boomed down the stairs, but it

sounded somewhat strained. "What was that racket? Oh, it's you, Constable. Fall in the gaboon, did ya?" The sneer with which Drackett addressed him made Josh bristle, but he forced himself to stay calm.

"Where were you last night, Drackett?"

"Last night? My, my, ain't we gettin' nosy? Guess you could ask Irma here, ain't that right, Irma?" Drackett waved his right arm in a sweeping gesture.

The girl only nodded, her pale skin ashen against her bright red dress.

"Are you through pokin' in my private life, Constable?" This time the sneer was accompanied by his teeth gritting.

Without waiting for Josh's reply, Drackett hooked his right arm through Irma's elbow and began to tug the girl back into the room behind them.

"Just a minute, Drackett," called Josh sharply. "I seem to recall taking a Colt off you over at Jersey Smith's."

"Yeah? Well, what of it? I ain't forgot, you little— But you can see I ain't wearin' one now." Drackett moved his right hip and side into Josh's view, and once again started to back up into the doorway.

"But, Mike," Josh corrected softly, "my recollection is that you are left-handed."

The girl called Irma screamed, as if some restraint had suddenly snapped. She pulled away from Drackett's grasp, stumbled, and fell to the floor, propelled by a rough push from her companion.

As he turned involuntarily, his blood-stained left side and bound up left arm came into view. So did the Starr revolver he wore in a cross-draw holster on his left side.

Drackett reached for the pistol as Josh fumbled with

the stock of the greener. The upward angle was awkward for the sawed-off shotgun. It was a toss-up which man could bring his gun to bear first, but Drackett's side was stiff and he was not that good with his right hand.

The Starr hadn't even cleared leather when the twelve gauge's deafening roar sent all the patrons of Fancy Dan's diving for cover. Eight of the nine double-aught pellets found their mark, and Drackett was hurled backward through the doorway behind him and into the bedframe. His torso folded back onto the bed, his legs draped on the floor.

———————

"Lower away," hollered Dub Taylor, shouting to make himself heard over the ringing sound of single jacks and the puffing donkey engine whose cables drew the ore cars.

Taylor was on his way down to gallery number five to inspect the condition of the working face. The lowest level of the Silver Rim had finally been pumped dry, and just last night Beldad had personally set the charges to begin the excavation.

As he rode deeper into the mine, the heat increased noticeably, and the walls became slick with moisture. *This sure enough reminds me of the Consolidated in Virginia*, he thought. *Now there was a bonanza—three or four levels of good assay that anyone would be proud to work, and then wham! Right in the middle of the hot, steamy water, the sweetest vein you ever saw. To think what they'd have missed if they'd never gone that deep!*

Far overhead, the operator of the cable saw the red painted stretch of steel cords appear that marked the level of the opening to gallery number five. Slowing the descent of the platform, the operator brought the moving floor to a stop even with a rocky ledge.

Taylor stepped off and walked forward in the curious step-pause-step gait of the long-time hard-rock miner. Underground, men didn't rush about, or the candle in the tin reflector mounted on their heads would blow out. Moreover, many a man had lived through a narrow escape by listening to the sounds of creaking timbers and rumbling earth in that brief delay between steps.

Taylor patted the sixteen-inch square box timbers that formed the framework of the mine's tunnels and shafts. Bending over, he paused to inspect the base of the timber which had been immersed in water the day before. It didn't appear to have been damaged, but for safety's sake it would need to be replaced. Dub wanted to see if work could continue on gallery five while new timbers were being put in. Beldad's blast the night before was intended to test the trustworthiness of the giant beams.

Beldad's shot, loaded and fired by him alone from much further away than the miners usually worked, was also expected to reveal something else. If level five showed promise, then Morris could begin rehiring additional miners. If, on the other hand, it showed poorly, then work would continue on three alone, and the single men would still be without jobs.

The flickering light of Dub's candle-lantern began to show pieces of rubble from the blast as he got nearer to the working face. As he turned a bend into what should have been a wider and higher gallery with a sloping mound of rubble ready to be cleared from the face, he stopped in consternation. The space was choked with debris. Boulders of all sizes blocked the passage and kept

Dub from even seeing, much less reaching, the far wall. "What in blazes is this?" he demanded of the heap of stone. "It looks like Beldad shot the roof instead of the face! He's completely blocked the gallery. We'll have two more weeks of work just to get it cleared."

Taylor turned, still muttering to himself, angry to the point of distraction as he thought about how quickly he'd like to fire Beldad and then wring his neck, or maybe the other way around. He was still disturbed as he kicked first one loose stone and then another. Why would Beldad do something so patently stupid and which benefited no one? Absentmindedly, Dub bent to pick up a chunk of rock.

He didn't even hear the hissing, crackling sound until he turned to see the flame moving up the cord to the ceiling of the tunnel ahead of him.

"Hey!" he shouted, "Hey! I'm in here!" He realized even as he yelled that the fuse was already burning too close to the charges to be pulled out in time.

A series of short, sharp concussions went off like brief claps of thunder. Dub was thrown against a rock wall, but wasn't knocked unconscious. He had just time enough to raise his hands to his bleeding ears before twenty-five tons of ceiling fell on him.

CHAPTER 14

"I say we lynch him—string him up."

"What cause did he have to blast old Mike thata-way?"

"It was Mike who bushwhacked Roberts the night before; that's how he got that wound on his left side."

"Yeah? Says who? That's what Roberts wants you to think, ain't it? He's had it in for Mike ever since he came to Garson. Besides, who said Roberts got bushwhacked? Did anybody see the other feller? And don't be handin' out that swill about Roberts bein' shot in the head an' all. A little bandage don't account for a head wound. How come *he* ain't dead?"

"But Drackett *was* shot in his gun arm—that's the only way Roberts could beat him at the draw."

"Who you gonna believe anyway, Mike or that boot-lick Roberts? Mike told me that somebody shot *him* from ambush."

"Hey, it coulda happened that way. What about the fellers who died suddenly? Like Swede—with his neck broke. In his whole life he never drunk so much he couldn't walk straight. How could he end up walkin' off a cliff?"

"Yeah, an' how about Dub Taylor? Mighty peculiar, that rock fall catchin' him all by hisself."

161

"Why would Roberts want to kill a foreman? I mean, they both work for Morris, don't they?"

"Yeah, well, maybe Roberts wants to run this whole town *and* the Silver Rim. I hear tell that since that blind gal is sweet on him, Morris'll do anything he wants."

"McGinty won't let 'em push us around. McGinty's as big a man as Morris, and he'll stand up to Roberts, too."

Beldad smiled contentedly and listened, while rolling a homemade smoke as he leaned back in his chair. He hadn't even had to stir this pot to make it boil. The out-of-work men were ready to believe the worst about Roberts. He was a handy target, since he represented both the management of the Rim and the law. All Beldad had to do was drop the suggestion that Roberts was looking for an excuse to murder Drackett, and the fuse of mob action was ignited.

McGinty will be pleased, Beldad thought, *and that spot as General Foreman is as good as mine. You did good, Mike. You didn't amount to much alive, but you made up for it in your death!*

———————

"I think," remarked Fancy Dan McGinty with evident satisfaction, "that we've got everything coming our way now. Don't you agree, Mr. Beldad?"

"Yes, sir, Boss, it sure seems that way—except for . . . except . . ."

"Oh, yes, the loss of your job at the Silver Rim. Think nothing of it, Beldad, uh, *Mr. General Foreman.* How does that sound to you?"

"Sounds great, Boss. But are you sure everything's been taken care of?"

"Second thoughts at this late hour? All right, Beldad, let's review: One, gallery five is buried under enough rubble that Morris and his men won't stumble on the big strike. But we can get it in operation in, oh, a week or ten days, since we won't waste any time on level three. Two, the Working Men are disrupting even the little production that the Rim still has, hastening the time when its stock will fall into my lap. Three, Pitahaya and his savages have gotten their promised rifles and will be able to take the next payroll shipment, no matter how well armed it is. That will be the finish of Morris, because none of his precious family men will continue working if unpaid. He'll be forced to concede defeat."

"Haven't you forgotten something, Mr. McGinty?"

"I don't think so. What's that?" McGinty replied easily, pulling out his watch to examine its polish.

"What about Roberts?"

"Didn't I tell you, Mr. Beldad? I'm sending up to Jawbone Canyon to bring back Logan."

"Miles Logan?"

"The same. The man they call 'Gates of Hell.' And that, Mr. Beldad, should put a finish to any concern we have with Joshua Roberts, once and for all."

"Josh, I've something I need you to do. I'll tell you now that I don't feel good about asking you, and I'll understand if you refuse."

"Mr. Morris, I never went looking for this constable's job, but once I took it, I never figured to turn down something because it looked hard. Tell me what you need."

"As you know, we've got to get the next payroll shipment here at once, or the Rim is finished. McGinty will certainly own it, and he'll be able to run this town as he sees fit. I don't think either of us wants that." At Josh's emphatic shake of his head, he continued. "I'm certain that the Mojaves are watching the line closely, and waiting to attack again when they know the gold is there. So even if I could get a party of armed men to guard the stage, that would only be a signal to the Indians that here was a coach worth attacking!"

"But they wouldn't try to hit a well-armed party, would they? I thought a quick raid against no defense was more their style," Josh interjected.

"Up until the last attack on the coach, I would have agreed with you. But some things have changed. The Mojaves have figured out that the army is occupied elsewhere. They may be trying to get enough gold to retreat across the border to Mexico in between Apache-style forays. Even worse, they have gotten hold of some repeating rifles."

"Yes, so I hear. They must have stolen them from the prospectors they ambushed."

"That's what I assumed, but the stage driver and guard both say that as many as a *dozen* Mojaves were using them—poorly, I might add, but we can't trust poor marksmanship to continue. Besides, if someone is trading Winchesters to the Indians, the next coach may be facing twenty or thirty rifles!"

"What's the answer, then?"

"I've sent an urgent message requesting a detachment of cavalry be sent here at once. I have some friends in San Francisco with enough connections in Washington to get some prompt action. But 'prompt' in army terms means a couple of weeks, anyway. Right now we need to pay these miners, or all work on the Rim will stop."

"What does all this have to do with what you said you had to ask me?"

"I want you to ride as scout for the next coach. There will be just the driver and guard on board. With you riding ahead to look for signs of ambush, you should be able to give the stage enough warning to turn around, avoiding a fight altogether.

"The Mojaves won't expect us to ship gold without a string of guards, so a second coach will be hitched up and surrounded by as many men as I can hire. It will proceed to the edge of the most dangerous stretch, then fake a breakdown. If the Indians are watching as closely as I think they are, they won't want to give away their position by attacking you when they think the gold shipment is following close behind."

Josh nodded pensively. "Sounds like it might work. When do you want to try it?"

"Just as soon as possible. Hurry Johnson and his guard have agreed to drive if you're the scout. Seems they've heard about your reputation for coolness. Said they'd agree to it, if you would."

"And we'll be leaving—"

"Tonight. Under cover of darkness, going *away* from Garson, there'll be little chance of trouble with the Mojaves."

"All right sir. I'll go make ready. Oh, one more thing. Do you think I could say goodbye to Callie before I go?"

A smile broke through Morris' weariness, and there was a twinkle in his eye. "I thought you might ask, son. She's waiting in the other room."

———

"Boss, that stagecoach pulled out last night," reported Beldad to McGinty, who was shaving with an ivory-handed straight razor in front of a brass-framed mirror.

"So, what of it? We're not interested in coaches leaving Garson, only those coming in. Anyway, I've told the Indians that the next gold shipment will undoubtedly be heavily guarded. Now that they have the rest of the rifles, they're ready to attack at the first sign of valuables being shipped."

"Right, Boss. Uh— By the way, Roberts isn't in town neither."

McGinty turned around with his face still half-lathered. "*What?* How do you know?"

"Remember you told me to keep an eye on him on account of what we got planned for the Rim? Well, I had one of the boys ask if Mr. Roberts was at breakfast yet, and that old potato-eatin' biddy—sorry, Boss—that Mrs. Flynn said he wasn't in the place and hadn't been there since yesterday afternoon."

"What? Hold on, Beldad; let me think." McGinty turned back to the mirror and absently resumed shaving.

"It must mean something," he observed to his reflection in the steamy glass. "Old Morris may be more subtle than I give him credit for. He wouldn't part with Roberts just to send him to hire some guards. He must know that Roberts's presence has been keeping the lid on things here."

Beldad knew better than to interrupt McGinty's reverie. Besides, he was inwardly cursing his stupidity for making a disparaging remark about the Irish. He was so involved with hoping McGinty hadn't noticed that he missed it when McGinty addressed him again.

"Huh? What did you say, Boss?"

"Pay attention, Beldad. I think the time is ripe for all our plans to bear fruit. With Logan coming to town tonight, we're ready to shut down the Rim. By the time you get back, we'll have it all."

"Get back from where?"

"Didn't you hear anything I said? I want you to ride to Red Rock Canyon and tell the Mojaves not to be fooled by any guarded coach unless Roberts is with it. Tell them he'll be riding a buckskin horse and carrying a shotgun!"

CHAPTER 15

"I'm sure sorry we had to let on to those men that they weren't really guarding a gold shipment. I'm afraid some careless word might get back to the Mojaves." Josh voiced his doubts to Hurry Johnson as they hitched up his teams at Weidner's.

"Naw, it ain't likely. Gettin' in two nights ago, and jest hirin' them last night, and leavin' this mornin'—I figger it ain't had time to get to them savages. Besides, you can't blame them for not wantin' to face Injuns totin' brand new Winchesters for no twenty dollars."

"I guess you're right. But I wish we hadn't been here a day already. Are they ready to roll?"

"Same as us. They're gonna be just enough behind us that them Injuns will be watchin' both coaches. We don't want them to be hittin' us by mistake on account of not seein' the play-actin'."

Hurry's voice held a sad and regretful note. Josh caught it and asked, "What's the matter? Don't you think it'll work?"

"Yeah, it'll work, I reckon. But to keep from gettin' ahead of them fellers, I'm sure gonna have to drive slow!"

"What do you mean, stopping these miners from

going to work? By what right are you trespassing on Silver Rim property?" Morris was shouting at a group of men who were milling around in front of the mine entrance. They included a line of men carrying weapons and led by a man dressed in black.

"Well, I represent the Working Men of Garson, and they have picked me to be their spokesman—"

"You?" interrupted Morris. "You're no miner, and neither are these others with you. I see some *behind* you who used to work for me. You men, what are you doing with these hooligans?"

The man in black laid his hand on the butt of his pistol with a confident air. Several others in the line did likewise, but with less bravado. "I said I'm the spokesman, old man, so you'd best speak with me."

"All right, whoever you are, what do you want?"

"Are you prepared to give these single men, unfairly relieved of work, their jobs back?"

"Certainly not! Not only is it impossible for the Rim to support them now, but I would never give any man holding a gun on me a position in my mine—now, or ever!"

"Then we, the Working Men of Garson, are prepared to see that no one else works either, until we are treated fairly."

"We'll see about that! You just get—"

Morris's push forward and his brave words were cut short when the man in black drew his pistol and slammed its barrel into the side of Morris's head, knocking him to the ground.

"Tote his carcass out of my sight," the gunslinger ordered, "before I get really mad. And don't bother comin' to work until he either changes his mind or there's an owner with more sense at the Silver Rim. This mine is closed."

————

Just outside the mouth of Red Rock Canyon, Hurry pulled his team to a halt. Oliver got down off the box to check the rigging as Hurry stepped around for a word with Josh.

Josh had been riding inside the coach, with his horse, Injun, tied on and trailing behind. He and Hurry had decided to travel this way to keep the weight off Injun's back and keep him fresher for the time when his speed might mean the difference between life and death.

"Right here's where that other bunch will have their breakdown," observed Hurry. "I figger there's a Mojave watchin' us right now, but all he'll see us do is put out an outrider." Hurry squinted back across the alkali flats to where an approaching swirl of dust could be seen, "In about five minutes, that Mojave'll be talkin' about a whole mess of men and a coach with a busted wheel gettin' fixed, right here outside the canyon. Soon as the guards get in sight, you can saddle up and go to scoutin'."

Josh limbered the greener and checked its loads, thrusting some more shells into his shirt pockets from the cartridge pouch hanging from the saddle horn. He put the bit in Injun's mouth and flipped the bridle over the buckskin's head. Tightening the girth on the saddle, he untied the lead rope from the coach frame and mounted.

"I'll ride as far out front as I can so you can still see me. That will give you the most time to get turned if we've guessed wrong."

"Look sharp, boy. Them Mojaves ain't likely to show

themselves, so you'll have to be right good. Just don't come back toward the coach for a chaw or nothin', 'cause if I see you turn around before we get through this canyon, you'll be eatin' my dust clean back to Weidner's!"

————

When Morris came to he was lying in the parlor of his own home being tended by Callie. A concerned and watchful half-circle around him was made up of Ling Chow, Pickax and Big John Daniels.

"My head," groaned Morris. "What happened?"

"Easy, Papa, just lie still," urged Callie.

Morris grimaced with the pain and clenched his jaw as if steadying himself. When he opened his eyes again his expression told them he now remembered what happened. "What are the miners doing about this?" he demanded.

Big John shifted his great bulk uneasily, hoping Pickax would speak. When he didn't, Daniels replied, "They ain't doin' nothin', Mr. Morris. They's scared. Scared of them hired guns.'"

Now Pickax broke his silence. "Scared is right! Especially by that black-dressed snake, Gates of Hell Logan. He's a cold-hearted killer if'n ever there was one."

"But surely we can get enough men together to outnumber those thugs!"

"Yessir, we kin," said Big John slowly, "but—"

"But what?"

"There ain't nobody the miners will follow, leastwise not against Logan."

"I'll lead myself. I'm not afraid of Logan."

"Oh no you won't," said Callie firmly, pressing her father's shoulders back down on the sofa. "I won't let you go and get yourself killed. No mine in the whole world is worth that."

There was a tap at the front door. Ling Chow shuffled out to answer it, returning in a moment with his face set. Almost without moving his mouth he announced, "Mr. McGinty here." Fancy Dan stepped quickly into the room, doing a poor job of concealing the smirk on his face as he looked at Morris' prostrate figure.

"What do you want, McGinty?"

"I heard about your unfortunate labor problem, Mr. Morris, and I came to offer my assistance."

"Your assistance? You swine, you're behind all this if I know anything!"

McGinty held up a cautioning hand as Big John took a menacing step toward him. "Don't be hasty, Morris; hear me out."

"All right, John, let's hear what this . . . this swindler has to say."

"It's plain that you cannot operate the mine. Your own people won't attempt to cross the line of the Working Men. Why, they're down in town right now, talking about how they haven't been paid, and asking why they should risk their lives for you."

"They know they'll get paid. There's a replacement payroll on the—" Morris silenced himself abruptly.

"On the way now? Well, let's hope they don't run into any Indian trouble like the last time, eh? But even *if* they should get here with that payroll—" The heavy emphasis on the *if* made Callie shudder—"these miners aren't going to challenge armed men for the sake of a few dollars." He smiled briefly, coldly.

"Look, here's what I'm willing to do," he went on blandly. "I'm so confident that I can run this badly managed mine better than you that I'm willing to buy your shares of Golden Bear Stock right now. That'll give me a place on the Board, which I will happily relinquish to the other directors in exchange for clear title to the Silver Rim. How's that for fairness? To take over a failing operation in the midst of a labor dispute, at a time when the town may be surrounded by hostile savages! You may call me crazy, but how does twenty-five thousand dollars sound, eh?"

Morris wavered for just a moment, weighing the offer. Then abruptly he made up his mind: "McGinty, get out of my house this instant!"

It was Callie who spoke next. She stood erect, facing McGinty as if her blind eyes nevertheless could see into his soul. "My father has poured his life into making this mine work and making this town a respectable place to live, to bring up families. Neither you nor your hired murderers will ever make us abandon the Silver Rim! Big John, show Mr. McGinty to the door!"

McGinty was already backing up as the giant black man advanced. "You'll regret this," Fancy Dan snarled; then he was gone.

"All right, Papa, now we know for certain who the enemy really is. What should we do now?"

"God bless you for your courage, child. Thank you for speaking out at just the right time. Now we need to pray for God to show us what is to be done."

"And pray for Josh's safe return?" asked Callie in a small voice, as if all the air had gone out of her slender frame.

"Yes, Callie, for that, too."

———

The plan must be working, thought Josh to himself with grim satisfaction. *Either that, or I have to suppose those Indians have given up their taste for stagecoaches after one try. And that I just don't believe.*

The sandstone walls rose plain and barren into the windless afternoon. Their pace through the canyon had been steady but unhurried, Hurry reasoning that to race through its snakelike turns might result in a spill that could prove fatal in more ways than one.

If Pick is right about the fighting Indians—and he is about everything else in this desert—then the prickles on the back of my neck mean we're being watched right now. Josh was watching the buckskin's ears closely, but while they were in motion, flicking back and forth, the horse's attention seemed more on the route up the canyon than toward the rocks on either side.

In a few moments Josh understood why. He reined Injun to a halt as the echo of hoofs coming toward him rebounded off the walls of the arroyo.

Josh glanced back over his shoulder; the coach was still coming along steadily. The guard was alertly scanning the cliffs to the sides and behind the coach, while Hurry watched ahead. *Nothing to do but keep on going,* thought Josh. *If I stop here, Johnson will think something is wrong even before I know what this is all about.*

Pressing the buckskin close against the side of the canyon that had a slight overhang, Josh cocked the greener and went warily forward.

Around the next bend came a lone rider. He too studied the canyon walls, twisting nervously in his saddle. Paying so much attention to the sandstone cliffs, he failed to notice Josh's approach.

When he did look up and recognize Josh, he nearly

spun the dun horse he was riding around. Mastering himself with great difficulty, he held up a trembling hand to halt Josh's progress.

Josh exclaimed, "Beldad! What are you doing here? Don't you know there's an Indian war on in these hills?"

"I . . . I . . . I came to find . . . find you," stammered Beldad.

"Came to find me? Since when have you—"

Just then the coach came into Beldad's view from around the last corner of the canyon before its walls opened out.

Beldad stood up in his stirrups and shouted, "It's here! It's here, you fools—this is the coach you want!"

————

Sotol had planted his ambush near the mouth of the canyon closest to the Garson side, hoping to lull the guards into falsely believing they had come through safely. He had let the first coach pass through without attacking it, so as to not give any indication of the presence of his band. When Beldad approached from the Garson road Sotol hadn't recognized him, and Beldad hadn't yet gotten up enough nerve to call out to the Indians he knew must be lurking nearby.

Across the canyon from Sotol's position, a young brave jumped to his feet and began firing wildly. One of the first shots knocked Beldad from his saddle; he hit the ground calling out miserably, "Not me, you idiots! Not me!"

Josh fired up at the cliff face, knocking down the Indian with a blast of buckshot. Over his shoulder he saw Hurry snap the reins to make his break through the canyon, now only a short distance away.

Confusion reigned among the Indians. They had been advised not to fire until the band of guards arrived and to remain completely still.

The Mojaves began firing their rifles, but the Indian Josh had killed was the last brave before the mouth of the canyon; the coach had, in fact, passed all but two of the ambush positions.

The stage raced ahead, and Oliver began firing with good effect, his booming shotgun forcing two Indian ambushers to take cover behind the rocks. The other braves had only the rear of the speeding coach for a target.

Josh spurred Injun ahead, then jerked him to a stop beside Beldad. Instinctively, Josh leaped from the saddle to drag Beldad out of the road just before the coach thundered by. Then he draped Beldad across the saddle, and leaping up behind him, encouraged his horse after the stage. A few badly-aimed shots rang out from the rocks, but they were soon out of range and danger.

At last the coach came to a halt, and while Oliver stood on the roof of the stage to watch their back trail, Hurry helped Josh load Beldad into the stage. He had been hit in the chest, and his breath came in short gasps.

Hurry looked at Josh, and shook his head. As they laid him on the passenger seat, Beldad's eyes fluttered open and he spoke to Josh with difficulty, "You . . . tried to save me. . . . I was trying to get you . . . killed!"

"By the Mojaves?" burst out Josh.

"McGinty . . . he and the Indians . . ." Beldad's back arched in a spasm of pain. His eyes widened, then glazed, and he was gone.

"You heard him, Hurry." Josh's voice was bitter, full of determination and anger.

"I sure did! I'd say we get on to Garson. McGinty's got a heap to answer for! And . . . look there!" Josh whirled in the direction Hurry was pointing and exhaled a long gasp of air.

CHAPTER 16

"I say we can't wait no more," Big John Daniels declared. "The longer we lets them gunmen stay, the tougher it's gonna be to get anyone to go up agin 'em. Besides, them mining company folks is liable to take McGinty's offer to buy the Rim just to get shed of all this mess."

"How many of them hired guns you figger there is?" Pick asked Big John.

"Well, we seen ten, counting that Logan, but three of 'em ain't really gunfighters. There could be more in the mine, but I doubt it. I ain't sure how many more Working Men there are in Garson, but they's just loudmouths an' out-a-work miners. They ain't killers."

"All right, then, let's go see what we can muster for our side. Lean Duck, you stay here with Mr. Morris an' Callie. Big John, you an' me best split up an' spread the word. Tell 'em to meet at the No Name in one hour."

———

At the prescribed time, at least fifty miners and townspeople were gathered at Jersey Smith's place. Two of the side canvas flaps had been tied up and back so as to accommodate the crowd.

Most already knew the situation, but at Big John's

call for action there was an uneasy silence. Finally a burly miner spoke up, "I'm right grateful to Mr. Morris for all he's done. But the reason I was still workin' is cause I have a family. And that family would rather leave here than have me dead. I ain't no hand to be facin' up to Miles Logan."

"Besides," said a single man, "I belong to the Working Men. I'm not sayin' hirin' those gunslingers was the right thing for McGinty to do, but this dispute's between him and Morris, right? I don't wanta get killed for either one of them."

When the man mentioned his connection with the Working Men, Big John started toward him with an upraised fist. Pick stopped him. "Easy there, Big John. We don't want to start any fightin' here—that won't get no mine back."

"An' you so-called Workin' Men," Pick said, "you listen up an' listen good. That's your side up there blockin' the road. Most of your group's up there now, herded together like so many cows. You'd best choose up sides pronto. This ain't no time to be watchin' which way the wind blows."

A few men backed out of the group and, with furtive looks behind them, skulked off up the road toward the mine.

"All right, here's the plan. We'll divide up into groups. Big John here'll lead one into the arroyo and up the wash behind where them fellers is blockin' the road. The second group'll go up the road and spread out along either side."

"Who's leadin' the second bunch, the ones goin' right into the teeth of them guns?" shouted a voice from the back of the crowd.

"Well," drawled Pick slowly, "it looks like I get that pleasant duty."

Shouts of "No" and "Sit down, old timer," erupted from the group.

"Some of those men are friends of ours," said a tall man with close-cropped brown hair, "and the others are hired killers. How can we fight that? I say we try to parlay with them."

There were murmurs of agreement and nodding heads.

"It won't wash," Pick replied. "Fancy Dan McGinty wants to keep the Rim shut down until he can take it away from Morris. I don't aim to let him do it."

"Then you'll get killed, Old Man," shouted another miner. "I haven't even been paid lately. Maybe McGinty could manage it better."

"Why don't you leave with them other skunks?" retorted Pick. "Sittin' here jawin' ain't getting work for nobody. I may be old, but I ain't yella!"

"What do you say, Big John?" asked the tall man who'd spoken earlier.

"I say we got to be men an' stand up for what's right. If talkin' would fix it, then talkin's jes' fine, but I say we go ready to fight!"

"Enough said," rejoined Pick. "Nobody's twistin' your arm, but if you're comin' with us, get your guns and let's go!"

———

Logan was lounging in the foreman's shack smoking a cigarette. A hired gun rushed in to warn him: "You better come, Logan; we got trouble."

Logan took another drag on his cigarette and tossed

it through the open door before leisurely getting to his feet. "Sonny boy," he replied, "we don't got trouble; we *make* trouble. Ain't you figured that out yet?"

"Yeah? Well, there's a bunch of armed men comin' up the road right now."

Logan drew his six-shooter and spun the cylinder, then replaced it loosely in its holster. He casually checked the leather thongs that tied it down to his leg before sauntering after the nervous young gunhand.

"Well, well, what *have* we here?" Logan spoke to Pick, who had halted with twenty others about thirty yards from the mine property. "You're an even older old coot than the last old coot who came up here. Ain't there any young folks who know how to talk in this town, or are you all played out?"

"Logan, we come to tell you to get outta here. You ain't wanted in this town."

"Is that it? And if I don't choose to go—how do you propose to make me?"

"Me an' these—" Pick began.

Before he could finish, Logan shouted, "Let's open the ball," then drew his Colt and blasted point-blank, putting a bullet through Pick's stomach and another into his side as the old prospector collapsed. Logan continued firing, joined by the other hired guns, until the miners and townspeople scattered to find hiding in the gullies and brush.

When the gunfire had ceased, Logan spoke again. "You men out there! Go on home, and there won't be any more killin'. Just don't cross me no more!"

A single miner came up behind Logan, who whirled around on him, the Colt pointed at the man's chest. The young man put both hands in the air, and swallowed hard. "We didn't want no killing, Mr. Logan. Not old Pickax, he—"

"Shut up before I plug you too! If you ain't with me right now, then I'll shoot you down where you stand."

"But I'm not even armed," sputtered the miner.

"Then you best run on back to that mine so's I can protect you, little squally brat. Now git!"

Rifle fire from circling miners and townspeople began erupting from the brush. The young Working Man needed no further urging; he and the other unarmed dupes of McGinty crowded into the mine entrance.

"All right," yelled Logan, dropping to cover behind an ore car, "give it to them!"

The armed thugs who began firing had chosen their protection better than the attackers. From behind the walls of the mine buildings and heaps of timber and mounds of ore, hired guns fired with deadly effect.

One of the attackers rolled over, wailing and clutching his shoulder. Another staggered up, holding his face in both hands, and fell over dead without making a sound. A third was hit in the hand.

None of the hired guns received so much as a scratch. "Go on home—all of you!" Logan called out again, "unless you're itchin' to die. That we can oblige."

A crackle of rifle fire mixed with the popping of smaller caliber pistols came from behind Logan's position. One of his men grabbed his leg and rolled on the ground cursing. Big John's group had succeeded in getting up the wash unseen and began another attack.

"You five—" ordered Logan, waving his pistol in a sweeping motion toward his gunmen on the front line. "Keep those rock-grubbers out there from moving up while the rest of us take care of the others."

Members of Big John's party were shooting steadily from the lip of the arroyo, but Logan's men still had plenty of cover from which to return the fire. Logan dashed from the ore car to a stack of timber. He fired three times over the stack, then retreated to calmly reload while a few shots struck the beams in reply.

Moving around the other end of the timbers, Logan dropped a miner who had just raised a rifle to his shoulder, then turned his aim toward Big John, who was brandishing a long-barrelled ten gauge shotgun. Logan's first shot clanged off Big John's shotgun as he brought it up across his face. The huge black man fell heavily to the ground, trying to conceal himself behind mesquite scrub one-quarter his size. Logan was aiming another shot at Big John's head when the ten-gauge blasted, and Logan dropped quickly to his belly.

General firing continued on all sides. The miners and townspeople had the greater numbers, but the skill of the gunfighters was winning the day.

The sound of pounding hoofs and the rolling, continuous creaking of a stagecoach at full speed drifted up from Garson between shots. Then the sound slowed but didn't stop, and the rushing noise continued right through town and up the hill toward the mine.

Hurry Johnson's rig rolled with such speed up toward the entrance of the Silver Rim that men from both sides of the fight had to throw themselves out of the road to avoid being trampled. When Hurry pulled the team to a halt, the leaders reared at the sudden stop. Behind the coach rode Josh on Injun. He was shouting and waving his hat, but no one could understand what he was saying.

When the team had quieted and the crowd stilled,

those who heard him were taken aback by the authority and urgency with which he spoke, "Stop this nonsense at once! Return to your homes; retreat to the mine buildings. Our only hope of survival is to band together."

"What? What are you talking about, Roberts?" One of Logan's men spoke up. "Is this some kind of cheap trick?"

"The Mojaves are preparing a full-scale attack on the town. At least fifty of them—maybe more!"

"That won't play, Roberts. Them Mojaves ain't got sand enough to make a try for a whole town!"

"That may have been true in the past, but now they're carrying Winchesters, and they're on their way here."

"Winchesters!" several gasped. "Where'd they get rifles from?"

"McGinty," was Josh's simple reply. "McGinty supplied them with all they'd need."

"My family! They're alone!" a miner cried out.

A single man from the entrance called out, "I'll come with you, Jim." A stream of men exited the mine, running for their homes and weapons to defend the town.

"What about us?" asked one of the gunslingers, shifting allegiance to the constable.

"Stay here and keep the road to town open. If necessary, we may have to all retreat back to the mine."

Before Josh could continue, he noticed Pick's body lying face down in the dust beside the road. His breath caught in his throat and he leaped from the buckskin to cradle the old man's head in farewell.

When he looked up, he asked bitterly, "Who's responsible for this?"

"Logan. Gates of Hell Logan."

"*Gates!* Where is he?" Joshua demanded.

Not even his own hired guns knew. In the sudden confusion at the entrance of the stage and Josh's announcement of the Indian attack, the man in black had taken the opportunity to escape.

McGinty pulled a .32 caliber pistol out of his desk drawer at the sound of footsteps pounding up the outside stairs to his office. He held it leveled at the entry.

The door burst open and Miles Logan almost fell in, panting. "The jig's up, McGinty. We've had it."

"What do you mean, 'had it'? Do you mean to say that you let this rabble of town clowns and dirty grubbers run you out?"

"No," gasped Logan as he struggled to catch his breath, "they're on to us—*you*, I mean. They know about the Indians and the rifles."

"What? How can they possibly know that?"

"Because," sputtered Logan, gesturing toward the sound of running feet pounding along the board sidewalks, "the Mojaves are coming to visit, and they're bringin' your calling cards with them!"

"Josh," Big John Daniels spoke quietly, "leave him for now. We gots a town to defend."

Josh made a pillow of his own hat and placed it gently under Pick's head, then he rose slowly to face Daniels. "All right. Let's go check on the Morris home."

"Good idear," Big John replied. Then he told Josh how Logan had beaten Mr. Morris with the butt of his pistol. Josh's jaw set grimly, the news giving him fresh determination to stop this madman.

———

At the Morris home, the two men hadn't even reached the front step when Ling Chow came rushing out. He held a shotgun under one arm, but the other dangled at his side, blood soaking his wide sleeve.

"Mr. Josh! God be thanked, you here!" the Chinaman burst out.

"What is it, Ling Chow, what's happened?"

"McGinty and man in black come here. They say they need . . . they need . . ."

"What? *Why* did they come? What did they say?"

"They say they need trade to buy freedom. They say no one follow till they send word or they will kill."

"Kill? Kill who, Ling Chow. You are making no sense."

Agitated and confused, Ling dropped the shotgun and grasped Josh's arm. "Why you not *understand*? They take Callie. *Callie*! They ride off in desert!"

"Callie!" Josh whirled Injun around, then stopped briefly to talk hurriedly with Morris before instructing Big John and Ling Chow in the defense of the house.

Morris himself lay on a couch with its back against an upstairs window, ready to defend the yard below. "Godspeed," he called hoarsely to Josh. "Please bring her home safely."

Josh nodded and was gone, pushing Injun to the limit up the winding trail that led past the Silver Rim and down through the canyons and washes to the desert floor below, even as the first sounds of gunfire drifted up from the town of Garson.

CHAPTER 17

As Josh rode furiously, his brain tried to sort out what he knew of tracking and what Pick had taught him of the desert trails. The thought of Callie's abduction and Pick's senseless death made him fearful and angry and his heels dug into Injun's side, spurring him on to greater speed.

What's happening to Callie? pounded through his brain. He hardly dared think of the danger she might be in. He could think only of finding her, making her safe again. He forced himself to watch the trail left by three horses—two side by side, and what seemed likely to be the prints of Callie's mare being led behind. If he thought of other things he feared he would miss a turn or mistake a sign.

Scanning the trail ahead, Josh was aware that Logan was too experienced a man to leave his back trail unwatched. So far, the kidnappers seemed to travel straight as an arrow. Intervening brush-covered hillsides blocked more than half-a-mile's view at a time. With each approach of the crest of a sandy hill, Josh skirted its rim so as to approach the backside from an unexpected direction. With no sign of any movement about, Josh regained the trail and rode on.

He knew they must go to water within another day;

they could not be carrying a greater supply than that. He trailed them until darkness forced him to stop for the night.

Josh hobbled Injun, and had a cold supper of jerky and hard biscuits from his saddle bags, washed down with water. He didn't want to take the chance of a fire revealing his position on the trail.

He could hear Injun contentedly chewing and rustling just outside the range of his night vision. Apparently the horse had found something to his liking, not returning to look for supper from his rider.

Josh took mental stock of his camp. His shotgun was at the ready and close at hand. Canteen and provisions were wrapped tightly in canvas, and stowed beneath his saddle, secured against marauding pack rats. The saddle served as his pillow. Calling goodnight to his horse, and breathing a prayer for Callie, Josh turned over, pulling half the tarp up over his muscular frame.

––––––––––––

The faintest gray in the east told Josh of the approach of dawn. He had slept fitfully and was eager to be off. Rubbing his eyes, a quick glance around revealed Injun standing not far off. In seconds he'd gathered his belongings together in a pile, and was striding toward his horse, bridle in hand.

As he walked, he observed that the stems of thin grass which his horse had been grazing were supplanted in places by clumps of a gray, hairy plant with long, spiky leaves. Here and there stalks of white flowers stood above the gray-green foliage. This must have been the plant agreeable to Injun, because he had chewed it down to the ground in places.

At his call, Injun lifted his head, and Josh approached the horse and stroked his nose and head. "Come on, boy, let's get movin'." The words, though spoken without urgency, had an unexpected effect.

Injun snorted violently and jumped sideways. "Easy, boy, easy. What's wrong with you? You got the jumps about something? Here now, easy."

Josh reached out again to stroke the horse's face and the animal appeared calm. *I wonder what that was all about?* Josh thought.

He flipped the loop of bridle over the horse's ears and began to place the bit in his mouth. Injun was trained to drop his head to allow the bit to be inserted, but he seemed to have forgotten this. He stood with his neck out-stretched and his head held unnaturally high.

Josh returned to camp and poured water into his hat for the horse to drink. After taking the water eagerly, the horse was more agreeable, letting Josh put the bit in his mouth. Leading him again to camp, Josh smoothed the saddle blanket on his mount and secured the saddle. Then he tied his blanket roll behind the saddle and looped the strap of the greener over the horn on the off-side. Tying the two canteens together, he hung them on the left side of the horn.

After a quick inspection, Josh jumped into the saddle and resumed the trail, hoping that Callie would be able to delay her captors as much as possible.

As Josh rode, the dawn breaking over the eastern hills began to light up the canyons and ravines to the west. From gray shadows, streaks of pink and orange began to appear as bands of brilliantly colored sandstone reflected the early morning rays. But Josh hardly noticed in his concern for Callie.

Soon the disk of the sun burst over the peaks. The warmth felt good on Josh's face, but it promised to be a very hot day. The night chill was nearly gone, and the sunlight had reduced the pale frost on the ground to white westward-pointing streaks shielded by the clumps of brush. In between the bushes, the ground was drying and beginning to steam.

Injun was still unusually agitated. His ears were constantly in motion, as if searching for danger nearby and confused at not finding it. His easy, ground-covering lope was interrupted frequently by sudden shifts to a bone-jarring trot. He could be urged back to the lope, but would again break its gentle rhythm without warning.

After about an hour of this annoying pattern, Josh stopped the horse to inspect his feet. Even though he had not been limping, Josh thought perhaps a hoof was giving him trouble. He soon located and dislodged a pebble from the hoof, and when he mounted again, Injun seemed to have a smoother gait. Josh fretted over the delay, regretting the time lost from his pursuit.

Then all at once Injun shied violently, sending Josh sideways in his saddle, almost dislodging him. The horse made three jumps over clumps of mesquite before Josh hauled up on the reins and shouted for the horse to stop. With the halt, Injun stood shuddering in place.

Josh patted the horse's neck and spoke soothingly to him. The horse's shuddering subsided, and Josh urged him back on the path once again.

Suddenly something white caught Josh's eye on the trail. Drawing up alongside it, he recognized it as a woman's handkerchief. *Good girl, Callie!*

With another pat to reassure his mount, Josh climbed down to retrieve the scrap of linen, keeping his fingers entwined in the bridle.

As Josh breathed in the scent of Callie's perfume, the horse gave a lurch backward, tumbling Josh to the ground. He cried out in pain as his elbow struck a sharp rock and he lost hold of the reins.

Rubbing his elbow, he reached for the trailing reins, but at the same moment Injun whirled, lashing out with both feet and nearly connecting with Josh's face.

"Hey! Calm down!" Again the animal was quiet, but as soon as Josh reached for the reins, Injun moved off, trotting a few more yards and stopping again to look back at Josh.

Josh mused. The stop-and-go game continued for three more attempts, but no amount of coaxing, wheedling, or threatening would make the horse stand still for Josh to grasp the reins.

Josh stood in the middle of the trail at a loss to figure out the problem. Then he used another tactic. As soon as the movements of the horse's ears and tail momentarily stopped, Josh made a rush for the trailing reins. But at the exact moment his fingers touched the leather, he stumbled over a rock on the trail and fell face-first in the dirt.

The fall was fortunate, however, because Injun had at the same time aimed another kick at Josh, which whistled over the top of his head. Then the horse was gone, running flat out down the trail, and disappearing over a small knoll about half a mile ahead.

The full horror of the situation washed over Josh. Not only had he lost all hope of overtaking Callie, but his bedroll, shotgun, and canteens of water were disappearing along with his horse, out of sight and out of reach!

The horse's abrupt departure left Josh some thirty

miles from the nearest water. It would have been a hard day's ride; now it was going to be a punishing hike.

Josh could only hope the horse would stop to graze, enabling him to catch up somehow. At least he appeared to keep to the trail.

Nothing was to be gained by waiting, so he started off down the faint path. As he went, Pick's words echoed in his ears: *A man in the desert without horse or water is a dead man.*

When Josh topped the next rise he could see Injun, not a quarter of a mile away, grazing just to the side of the trail. He plodded on toward the horse, trying to plan his strategy as he went. *I need to come up on his left to have the best shot at grabbing those trailing reins*, he reasoned. *And I can't spook him before I get that close.*

He decided to mimic the horse's own actions as a means of putting the beast at ease. Each time the horse lifted its head to gaze around, Josh stood still and bent to the ground, even plucking a handful of the thin grass. Moving forward only when the horse grazed, and stopping when it lifted his head, he was able to approach within a few yards of him. The next time Injun raised and turned his head, Josh shook a handful of the grass, and called gently, "Look here, boy—see what I have for you."

The horse flared its nostrils suspiciously, and when Josh didn't move, stretched its neck toward him.

Injun had been standing sideways to Josh's approach, but now he turned to face him directly. Stretching out his neck again he sniffed at the grass, deciding whether to investigate the offering.

Josh took a step closer and the horse snorted, but didn't move. Extending the bouquet without moving another muscle, Josh stood completely still, silently praying.

Injun nudged the grass with his nose, and took another step forward. Josh held his breath. If only he could wrap both arms around its neck, then secure the reins. The whole scene was so incredibly bizarre.

The horse pulled away again, as if reading Josh's thoughts. Slowly, agonizingly, Josh began to inch forward again with the bundle of drying weeds, willing the horse to lean closer. He arched his left leg, fearing to step forward, lest he frighten the horse away.

At six feet apart Injun stopped. Josh gingerly pushed the fistful of drooping grass stems out. The horse stretched his neck to its greatest length, and then as if this were not safe enough, proceded to nibble the weeds with only his lips. Injun's ears flicked nervously back and forth. A tremor began in his withers and ran down through his flank. *He's getting ready to bolt*, thought Josh anxiously. *It's now or never.*

As if reading his thoughts the horse exploded into motion, whirling to its left, and pulling the reins out of Josh's reach.

Lunging for his neck, intending to hold on for all he was worth, Josh stumbled forward and Injun reared. A flailing hoof glanced off Josh's shoulder as he ducked to the side.

Josh leaped for the horse's side, thinking he could perhaps drag himself into the saddle. His hands felt the shotgun hanging from the horn, and he grasped it. The horse reared again, lashing out with iron-shod hoofs and twisting again to the left.

For a moment Josh could feel the horse being pulled toward him. Seconds later, the leather sling on the greener parted from the stock with a crack like a whip.

A wild flurry of flying hoofs was followed by a buck that brought Injun's head completely to the ground. One murderous kick aimed at Josh's face, and the horse was gone, pounding away to the west. Josh was alone again, holding the greener with its dangling, broken strap.

CHAPTER 18

For two hours he tracked the horse into the relentless afternoon sun. Once he came within a hundred yards, but that was the closest point before Injun made another dash away.

Dear God, help me, Josh pleaded. He continued to trail his only hope for survival into the dusty, still, desert afternoon. His mouth was dry and the skin on his face became stiff and taut. The moisture was leaving his body. As lack of water in the blazing heat took its toll, his mind began to wander and his steps faltered.

He began to pick up small pebbles from the trail to put in his mouth to start the saliva flowing. In his delirium he found himself spending a long time choosing the stones. Hours passed, and Josh could feel his life ebb away with the moisture. A thick, pasty film formed on his palate, causing him to gag and retch.

The shotgun trailed over his shoulder by its broken sling, and the stock bumped against his back causing increasing irritation. At one point he was tempted to whirl it around his head and fling it into the brush. He interrupted his frustration in time to allow the weapon to swing to a stop.

Then he tried to tie the end of the leather strap through the trigger guard to make a loop again, but found that his brain would not communicate the necessary steps to his fingers to tie a knot. He wandered aimlessly down the path, his feet keeping to the trail while his mind and hands fiddled with the problem.

A dry wash cut across the landscape in front of him. Its drab brown and ashen color blended in with the surrounding plain, and he didn't see it until almost too late. Half-sliding, half-swinging around a Joshua tree saved him from falling.

There, just below him in the wash and pawing anxiously at the sandy bed, stood Injun. They both caught sight of each other in the same instant.

The horse whirled again to run but was slower now, awkward and struggling. The relentless sun had taken its toll on his mount as well. The greener was already in Josh's hands. He instinctively brought it to a tight grip against his side and his right hand thumbed back the hammer. There was a deafening roar and a cloud of bitter gray smoke.

Josh dropped the gun and ran into the gully, tumbling head over heels as he went. He came up next to the still form of Injun. A quick look told him that the double-ought had done its work—the horse had dropped down dead and never moved again. But in spinning, rearing, and falling, Injun had come down heavily on his left side. The double-yoked canteens had been crushed beneath him, and as Josh wrenched them free from beneath the carcass, the last drops were being swallowed up by the thirsty sand.

Flinging himself face-first into the dust and gravel of the gully, Josh tried to suck life-giving water from the moist sand. He came up sputtering and retching as the harsh alkali soil burned his mouth and throat. The earth must have been even drier than Joshua, because it leeched the last moisture from his mouth, leaving him worse off than before.

Joshua knew he was in the most desperate situation possible. It was best that he act in anxious haste, because otherwise he might not be able to act at all. Reaching into his pocket, he drew out a small, folding knife. With a crushed canteen held as a bowl under Injun's neck, Josh stabbed downward fiercely and slit the horse's throat. Bright red blood gushed out, flooding the canteen, Josh's hands, and the ground. After a moment's hesitation, he drank. Forcing down his rising gorge with difficulty, he swallowed and swallowed again, until the bowl was empty. The blood flowing from the dead horse was now only a trickle, but he refilled his improvised bowl. When it was full, he drank it all down again, every drop.

Josh looked at his gore-covered hands. Then he looked at the crimson pool shrinking rapidly into the sand and clotting into blackening clumps. His mind flashed a picture of how his face must look—mouth ringed with blood, and chin and shirt spattered with it. He dropped the canteen and threw his hands up to his face in horror and revulsion.

Josh had to rouse himself from the desire to lay back and rest. He had to continue on in search of Callie. *Callie!* Her face flashed across his brain like lightening leaping to a peak in a Sierra thunderstorm. He had pursued the horse and the canteens for a whole afternoon, gradually forgetting why he was out in the desert in the first place.

God, he thought, *I'm going crazy. I think I hear her voice calling my name.*

"Josh, is it you? Josh, answer me!"

Callie! Then he heard McGinty and Logan. He *had* found them. Or was it the other way around?

"Ain't you a sight?" chuckled Logan. He casually drew his Colt.

At the rustling of the gun from its leather, Callie pleaded, "No, wait! Please don't hurt him!"

"Well, now, pretty lady, just since you ask. I just wish you could see your hero, gettin' hisself a fine drink of horse blood."

Turning to McGinty he added, "Shall we jest leave him out here to find his own way back? Maybe someone will rescue you, like the first time I left you in this predicament," he sneered at Josh.

"Gates," Josh groaned hoarsely, trying to make his brain, fuzzy with dust and sun, to work. *How can I get Callie away?* he pondered.

"Let's get going, Logan. Bring Miss Morris and come on," ordered McGinty.

"You know, Roberts, it wasn't too smart of you to go blastin' off with that cannon yonder. Not with us sittin' just the other side of this gully. Not smart at all."

"I wouldn't be too sure about that," came another voice from the edge of the wash.

Rather than waste time looking to see who spoke, Logan spun on his heels and fired the Colt in the general direction. Such a move may have worked had there been only one man to deal with. But *three* men stood on the rise. Before Logan made a full turn, Nate Dawson's .45 cut him down and Logan's shot went wild. Callie Morris screamed.

Tom Dawson never flinched. He kept his gun on Logan a moment longer, gesturing for Nate to walk cautiously down from the opposite side of the gully. He approached carefully in case the gunman was shamming, but Miles Logan was dead.

"Miss Morris, Tom Dawson here. Don't worry; everything's under control. Mont is holding a gun on Mr. Fancy Dan McGinty."

Callie didn't wait any longer. She cried out as she ran toward Josh, calling his name.

"Here, Callie! I'm here, love!"

She flew to him, throwing her arms around his neck. Holding each other was enough.

Josh tried to hold her back, saying, "No, Callie, I'm all over blood!"

Callie stopped only a fraction of a second and, as Josh wiped his face on his sleeve, she scolded, "Joshua Roberts, what's a little blood as long as it isn't yours?"

"Come on, you two," Tom called after he figured an appropriate time had passed. "We'll take Mr. McGinty with us while Nate and Mont bury Logan."

"I guess I can take Logan's horse," Josh commented. "He won't be needing it any more."

"Sounds good," said Tom. "The others are a mite frisky, even for a salty old desert hand like yourself."

"Others?" Josh asked, looking around.

"Just up ahead," Tom indicated. "This wash leads up to the box canyon where we round up the mustangs before driving them to Garson. There's water there, but none of that loco weed for the horses to get into. Drives 'em crazy, you know."

EPILOGUE

"Yes, Papa, I'm just fine. Better than you, I think," Callie assured him.

"If you feel up to it, sir," urged Josh, "tell us what happened in the Indian attack."

"Wasn't anything to it at all," said Morris, his head wrapped in bandages. "Those Mojaves weren't expecting a whole town full of armed folks, and mad besides! For all their Winchesters, they couldn't stand up to the citizens pulling together and fighting it out like real soldiers. The only real damage done was by a fire. Quick work saved the other businesses, but not before Fancy Dan's place was gutted. Anyway, I've heard that the army detachment is on the Mojaves' trail and will chase them clear to Mexico if need be."

"And the mine, sir—can you save it from being closed permanently?"

"That's the best part. I sent Sexton into the Silver Rim to see if those hooligans had damaged any equipment. He brought up a specimen of rock from gallery five's collapsed roof. You won't believe what he found."

"What's that, sir?"

"The sample assayed out a thousand dollars a ton! Sexton says it probably gets richer behind the rockfall. Of course McGinty knew about the rich vein, and Beldad was working to keep it a secret till McGinty owned the Rim. I've already telegraphed the news to the other directors, and they've agreed: everyone goes back to work."

"That's wonderful, Papa!" exclaimed Callie. "Now the town can grow—be a place to raise families and—" She stopped, blushing suddenly.

Both men laughed, and Callie joined in. "But you have to promise me one thing, Papa," she continued. "That the Rim will donate land and money to build a church."

"Whatever you say, my dear. Sounds like a very good idea to me." He turned to Josh. "Seem reasonable to you, constable?"

"I think we still need a jail, first," he countered.

"Why, Joshua Roberts, how can you say such a thing?" Callie protested.

"Well, actually I was just quoting what Fancy Dan McGinty is probably saying."

"McGinty? Why do you say that?" Morris questioned.

"Because he's out there right now, chained to that T-rail," gestured Josh, pointing out the window toward the bustling activity of the Silver Rim.